INSPIRED BY FROST

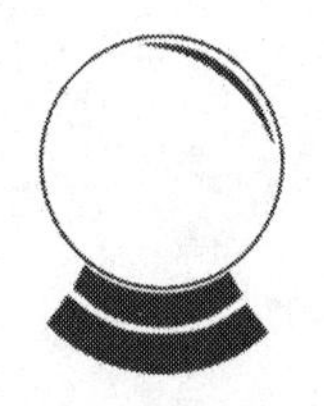

CRYSTAL FROST BOOK THREE

ALICIA RADES

This is a work of fiction. Names, characters, places, and incidents are either the product of the author's imagination or are used fictitiously, and any resemblance to actual persons, living or dead, business establishments, events or locales is entirely coincidental.

Published by Crystallite Publishing.

Produced in the United States of America.

Cover design by Clarissa Yeo.

ISBN: 978-0-9974862-1-6

To my mother-in-law, Deb, who constantly encourages and inspires.

1

My fingers quivered as I reached for the dress's zipper and a wave of nausea hit me. I closed my eyes and took a deep breath, hoping the dizziness would pass. The dressing room spun around me, and I braced myself against the bench in the corner for support. I opened my eyes and fixed them on a spot on the floor. Then the realization of what was happening hit me.

Not again, I thought. *Not now.*

The last few months had been fairly passive as far as my psychic abilities went. I had been practicing how to use them in case something like this happened again, but to have it happen now of all times was a bit of a shock. I was becoming a better psychic, and I had almost fully mastered the little things, but I still didn't know how to control my body when a ghost came around.

I lowered myself to the bench. The lavender dress still hung loose around my shoulders. I took a deep breath to steady myself, and when I looked up, there she was.

I could tell she was dead, partly due to the feeling I was getting. The other reason I knew she was dead was because I could see straight through her like she wasn't entirely there. Judging by how transparent she was, I knew she didn't have much time.

She had long brown hair, but nothing about her was particularly striking. I probably wouldn't remember her if I saw her on the street.

"Crystal?" she asked.

I didn't know how, but whenever a ghost came to me for help, he or she always knew my name and could tell that I could see them.

I wanted to help her. I always wanted to help anyone who came to me, but I was hoping I could enjoy a day of shopping with my mom for my maid of honor dress without any interruptions. Now that she was here, though, I couldn't push her away, not when she needed my help.

"What?" I managed breathlessly in almost a whisper so no one else would hear.

"My name is Melissa," the girl said. "And I need your help."

I swallowed. "How? How can I help you?" I tried to keep my tone as friendly as I could, but it came out sounding more urgent than I wanted it to.

"You need to save her."

"Save who?" Ghosts always had this way of telling me what to do without actually telling me what to do.

"Sage."

Sage? I didn't know any Sage. How could I help someone I didn't even know? I knew that fact alone would make this mission difficult.

"Sage Anderson," Melissa clarified.

"How? How can I save her? What's wrong with her?" I kept my voice to a low whisper.

Melissa blinked and shook her head in sadness. "She's too young. I don't want her to suffer the same fate."

"Huh?" was all I could say.

Then Melissa's eyes locked on mine. "If you can't save Sage, she's going to die. She'll take her last breath the next time you wear that dress. That is, unless you can save her."

My breath caught in my chest the same moment Melissa vanished. Something about her words, the way they seemed so final, told me she wasn't coming back. That was the first and last time I would see her.

A million questions raced through my head. *Who is Sage? How is she going to die? How can I save her? Will I be able to save her?*

A knock at the dressing room door startled me from my thoughts.

"Crystal, are you okay? What's taking so long?" my mother asked.

"Yeah," I called back, my voice wavering. I took a quick breath to calm my nerves. "I'm fine. I just . . . I can't reach the zipper." I unlocked the dressing room door and held it open a crack. "Can you help me?"

My mom pushed her way into the dressing room. It was a tight fit, but we were both small people. She was dressed in her regular jeans and tee since she'd already picked out her dress weeks ago. Now, with only four weeks left until the wedding, it felt like we were getting down to crunch time. It's not like the wedding was going to be huge or anything. It was just going to be family and close friends at one of the hotels here in the city.

My body shook slightly as my mom zipped up my dress and I thought about a girl whose life supposedly depended on me. I tried not to let it show, and even though I was always bad at hiding things, I didn't think my mother noticed my unease.

"How does that feel?" she asked once she had my zipper up.

I smoothed down the fabric and took a look at myself in the mirror. The dress had a tank-style lace top with a ribbon around the waist. The skirt fell just above my knees. It looked so good on me that I hardly noticed my nonexistent hips and flat chest. Best of all, the lace top complemented my mother's gown.

"I love it," I told her, but Melissa's words still echoed in my head. *She'll take her last breath the next time you wear that dress.* That meant that if we went with this one, I had until the wedding to save a girl I didn't even know. A mere month's time didn't seem like enough. "But, I don't know," I added. "Maybe we should keep looking." It didn't seem right to wear this dress and seal in Sage's fate.

"Well, come on," I heard Sophie's voice from outside the dressing room. "Let's see it on you!"

My mom and I emerged from the changing room. I glanced through the shop windows. The sun hung low in the sky. Since Mom ran a business with Sophie and Diane, her two best friends and bridesmaids, we had to go shopping when their shop was closed and everyone could get together away from work. On a normal day, the setting sun might bring thoughts of Robin to my mind and make me wonder how much time I would have to spend with him tonight before my curfew. But today, the setting sun only made me feel like time was already running out to save a girl I didn't even know.

Sophie and Diane were wearing the same dress I was. I eyed them and couldn't help but wonder if they could somehow assist me before it was too late for Sage. Like me, mom and her friends were all psychic. It's how they became friends in college and ended up opening their Halloween-themed shop, Divination, in my hometown.

Maybe, I thought, *they can help me figure out what Melissa meant and who she was talking about.* The thing was that in the past when they'd tried to help—like when I'd found a little girl named Hope who'd been abducted—they couldn't see anything about the situation. It was like the universe wanted me to do it all on my own.

"I like them," Diane said, twirling around in her own dress. She was a bigger woman, but the dress still looked great on her. In fact, it looked fantastic on all of us.

"It looks like we've found the one," Sophie agreed.

They both admired their new wedding attire in the full-length mirrors on the dressing room doors. I followed their gazes and noticed my fallen face. We couldn't choose this one, could we?

She'll take her last breath the next time you wear that dress.

If I never wore this dress again, that would mean she wouldn't die, right? I tried to put on a smile, but I wasn't sure how successful I was at it. *Should I tell them? Is it worth ruining this special day?*

Sophie turned to me. "Crystal, are you okay?"

I was never good at hiding my emotions with anyone, but it was impossible to hide behind a smile in front of Sophie. She was an empath, which meant she could feel other people's emotions and influence them.

I felt the tears stinging at my eyes already. I bit my lip to hold them back, but I couldn't help it. I flung myself into Sophie's arms and let a tear fall down my cheek. I shook my head. "No," I answered. "I'm not okay."

Suddenly, everyone was at my side. I didn't know

where the lady who was helping us earlier went, but right now, it was just me, Mom, Sophie, and Diane, and I was grateful for that. I needed the privacy.

"Sweetie, what's wrong?" my mom asked.

Everyone went quiet for a beat while I composed myself. After I released Sophie, she led me over to one of the nearby chairs and sat me down.

I took a deep breath. "It's happening again. I—I saw someone in the dressing room."

They all exchanged glances, looking for something to say. My mother knelt beside me and took my hand. "It's okay. You can tell us."

I nodded. I knew that much. It was a secret we all shared together. The thing was that I was the only one of all of us who could see ghosts. It felt like an overwhelming responsibility.

"She said her name was Melissa. She warned me that someone was going to die and that I needed to help her. I really don't want to see someone die if there's something I can do about it." I didn't add what I really wanted to say: *I'm terrified.*

"Sweetie, you know we're always here for you, right?" my mom said.

I nodded again, but I knew there was meaning behind those words that she wouldn't voice aloud. They were there for me emotionally, but their abilities couldn't help me.

"Did she say anything else?" Diane asked.

I nodded again and spoke so softly that even if

someone was close by, they wouldn't overhear. "She said that the girl who needed help was named—"

"How are you ladies liking that dress?" a voice interrupted. The woman who was helping us before returned.

We all shifted to look at her. A girl a little older than me with dark red hair, pale skin, and freckles across her nose stood next to her.

"I'm terribly sorry," the lady said, "but I have a family emergency. If you need anything, you can ask Sage." The lady gestured to the young woman beside her.

My heart stopped.

2

I forced down the lump in my throat. This had to be the girl Melissa was talking about. I mean, how common is the name Sage, and why would I meet this girl here immediately after I received a warning if it wasn't her? I knew it was her and that if I didn't do anything, she was going to die.

Sage put on a friendly smile and introduced herself to each of us. I wasn't as good as Sophie was at it, but I could get feelings about people's emotions if I touched them. When Sage held out her hand to me, I rose from my seat and put on my best smile. I shook her hand, hoping to learn something from it.

I must have thought I would get all my answers right away, like how she was going to die, but all I got was a feeling of terror—her terror—when I touched her.

She was afraid of something or someone, only I didn't know what or who.

How are you going to die, Sage? I wondered. *How can I help?*

But what was I supposed to do? I couldn't tell her she was going to die and hope she'd let me know how. Surely, she wouldn't believe me, and it would only make things worse as far as my involvement went. I had to find some way to get close to her so I could investigate her impending death, except I had no idea how to do that.

Sage complimented our dress choice and made a few suggestions for accessories before I had a chance to fully process the situation. Diane seemed suddenly interested in what Sage had to say and led her over to a rack of sashes while asking questions. Diane shot us back a glance that said she was giving us privacy.

I returned to my chair, and my mom and Sophie stood on either side of me. "That's her," I whispered, stealing a glance at Sage. "The girl in the dressing room said Sage was going to die. That has to be her."

Sophie nodded in understanding. "I can feel her fear. She's afraid of something."

"I know," I agreed. "Only, I don't know what."

Sophie bit her lip. "Me, either."

My mother rubbed my shoulder sympathetically. "I'm sorry, but maybe I can give a bit of advice. She's about your age. Why not try making friends with her? You might find out a bit more."

"Yeah, but I don't know what to say to her." I pressed my lips together nervously and peered at Diane and Sage again. Diane was successfully keeping her preoccupied.

"Mom, Melissa—the ghost girl in the dressing room—said I have until the wedding to save Sage. Well, what she said is that I have until the next time I wear this dress. I don't think we should get these ones. Then maybe Melissa's prophecy won't come true."

Sophie shook her head. "I don't think it works that way. I don't think it will matter what dresses we get. The good news is that you have a clear timeline."

"*And* you know who the girl is," my mom added. "We'll try to help you the best we can, but when it comes to interfering with another psychic's mission, the rest of us are just normal people."

I understood all too well what she was saying. Each time the universe had picked me for a mission, none of them saw what I saw. Sure, they'd been helpful, and I'd learned a lot about my abilities from them, but I knew any new piece to the puzzle would have to come from me.

Then I realized something. They had all helped me with a séance before, and it had worked. What if we tried contacting Melissa to get more answers?

That seemed like a good idea, so I mentioned it to them. They both agreed that we could try contacting her when we returned home. I smiled, mostly to reassure myself I could do this but also because I was glad to have their support.

"Why not try to get some answers from Sage first?" my mom suggested.

"Okay," I agreed. "Just give me a few minutes."

I took a deep breath and rose from my seat. I casually strolled over to the jewelry and tried to make it look like I was interested in the earrings. What I was really doing was stealing glances at Sage and Diane. When it seemed like they were finally done talking about accessories, I cleared my throat.

"Um, Sage?" I asked.

"Yeah?" She smiled, but it didn't quite reach her eyes.

"I'm curious if you have any suggestions for jewelry." My voice wavered a little, but she didn't seem to notice.

"Oh, sure."

"I'm Crystal, by the way."

"Crystal. That's a pretty name."

I tucked a long strand of blonde hair behind my ear. "My boyfriend says my name is really special because it's like my first name is an adjective and my last name is a noun. Crystal Frost is my full name."

Sage tilted her head slightly. "He's right. That is really cool." She held out a pair of earrings to me. They dangled and were adorned with a purple gem atop a pearl. "These would look great with your dress. We also sell a matching necklace."

I lightly touched the owl necklace hanging around

my neck. It was the one Teddy had given me when he proposed to my mom. I rarely took it off. I knew it was kind of dumb, but I felt like it gave me good luck.

"I already have a necklace in mind for the wedding," I told her, "but I really like the earrings."

"Do you want to see them on you?" she offered.

"Really?"

"Sure." She held them up to me.

I placed them in my ears and looked into the mirror next to the jewelry. "I really like them."

Hopefully I was connecting with her on some level. I wanted to see some indication of how I was going to save her, but I knew I couldn't push it. The universe had a way of showing things to me when it thought I was ready. Still, I couldn't help but want the answers right away.

"So, uh, this must be a pretty cool job, huh?" I asked. "You help women pick out dresses and accessories. It's like every girl's fashion dream."

Sage gave a light laugh. "Not really. I'm just saving up money for after high school. It's kind of tough since I only work on the weekends, but it's something."

"Well, you're lucky your job probably pays well," I said. "All I have is a babysitting job that pays only a few dollars an hour." I didn't bother mentioning that I loved babysitting Hope and would probably do it for free, but I was mostly aiming to find a common element between us. Perhaps that would give me a reason to talk with her more and learn more about her predicted death. When she didn't say anything, I tried another route. "Apart from that, I'm usually busy with extracurricular activities. Do you do anything fun at school?"

She shook her head. "No, not really."

"I play volleyball in the fall, and I'm in the band. I play clarinet. You don't play anything?"

She shook her head again. "I, uh, used to, but not anymore. But I still like music."

Disappointment washed over me. How much more could I say before I only pushed her away? Maybe I could fake a dress emergency during the week and come back here. Wait. That wouldn't work because she said she only worked on weekends.

But music . . . I might be able to work with that. "My boyfriend is in a band. Not the school band like me. They're more into pop, but they write their own songs. You should check them out sometime. They're actually going to be playing at my mom's reception."

Sage shrugged. "There are some local bands I've been meaning to check out, but I don't know. I don't really have the time." She bit her lip nervously like she wasn't telling me the whole truth. I got the feeling it was about whatever she was afraid of.

"Maybe you could give me your number and I could text you when their next performance is," I suggested.

"Oh, uh, I don't mean to be rude, but I don't really give out my number."

"I understand," I said as kindly as I could, but I was

actually disappointed.

"But you seem really nice," she said with a shy smile. "I guess it wouldn't hurt to actually get out once in a while."

I grinned, perhaps too excitedly. I would be able to see her again and maybe get some more answers! At the same time I got excited about getting her number, I realized that it was too easy. I could only wonder what would go wrong later.

3

My first indication that something was wrong happened when we got in the car. We had purchased our dresses, and Mom had even bought me the pearl earrings. I slipped my phone out of my pocket and opened the Facebook app, hoping to learn more about Sage on her profile. I found a few other Sage Andersons online, but based on the profile pictures, none of them were her. I tried Twitter, Pinterest, and Instagram but didn't find a single profile matching the girl I'd met in the bridal shop. I even turned to Googling her name, but all I came up with was the social profiles of other girls whose pages I already looked at.

How could a girl about my age *not* have a Facebook account? Or maybe her profile was buried beneath all the other results. I hadn't realized Sage was a common name, let alone that there was more than one Sage Anderson in the world. I tried narrowing my search but still couldn't find her.

Then a thought hit me. What if the Sage I met at the bridal shop wasn't the girl I was supposed to save? What if her last name wasn't Anderson and I was focusing on the wrong person? What if one of the Sage Andersons showing up in my search was the girl Melissa warned me about?

No, that didn't seem right. It had to be the girl in the bridal shop. No matter how long I thought about it, I couldn't come up with a clear answer.

Robin and I had planned to hang out after my shopping trip since I was already in the city and that's where he lived, but I called him disappointedly and told him I couldn't make it. I didn't tell him about Sage yet because I hoped I would have more answers after we tried contacting Melissa.

Robin and I had been dating since our trip to Florida last Thanksgiving when I rescued Hope and learned about Robin's car accident that led to his prosthetic leg. Our relationship was somewhat odd because his uncle Teddy was engaged to my mom, so in a few short weeks we'd technically be step-cousins, but we'd long gotten over that fact, and no one else seemed to mind since we weren't blood related.

But I couldn't hang out with him right now, not when a girl's life depended on me. He didn't ask me why I couldn't come over, but he did ask if I was alright.

"I'm fine," I told him honestly. "After we finished shopping, we realized we had something else to do, and it's not something that can wait until the wedding."

He seemed to understand even though I wasn't telling him the whole truth. I wasn't exactly lying to him either, but I didn't want to worry him.

After I ended my call with him, I found Emma's number in my contacts. She was my best friend and knew about my abilities, too. Emma had even been trying to channel her inner psychic over the past few months and was getting really good at it. The way my mom put it, Emma didn't have a natural connection to the other side like I did, but since everyone is mildly psychic, the work she'd put into practicing had made her a bit more psychic than the average person. I told her briefly about Melissa and Sage and that we were holding another séance.

"That's so cool," Emma raved. She was always excited when I brought up anything related to the paranormal, and she had taken it upon herself to research the crap out of anything supernatural. We even had regular practice sessions together. I knew Emma probably wanted Derek to join us, but even after all this time, he was still a bit of a skeptic.

When we arrived home, the house was empty. Teddy had said that since we'd be gone anyway, he might as well work the weekend at the station. Even though Mom and Teddy weren't married yet, he'd completely moved in a few months ago.

I hung up my lavender dress in my closet, which felt oddly depressing thanks to Melissa's warning. It wasn't supposed to be like this. Picking out my maid of honor dress was supposed to be fun. I lingered at my closet door for a few seconds, staring at the dress. *But it will be worth it,* I thought, *if I can save her.*

I forced my gaze off the dress and headed back to the living room. On my way out of my room, I caught a glimpse of my crystal ball on my dresser. I made a mental note to try that later if the séance didn't work. Sadly, crystal ball gazing was one of the skills I still couldn't quite get down.

Mom already had candles placed around the kitchen table. When I walked into the room, I made a note of how there were six chairs around the table but there would only be five of us conducting the séance. I wondered briefly what it would be like if Teddy filled that empty chair.

When I first found out about my—and my mom's—abilities, Teddy didn't know either. I'd helped Mom tell him, and he seemed accepting of it. Only later did I find out that he had a heightened sense of intuition, a type of psychic power, although it wasn't as strong as the rest of ours. I wasn't entirely sure what Teddy was capable of, but the way I understood it, he and Emma were at about the same level. They were both believers with mild abilities.

I still couldn't pinpoint why there were so many psychic people in my life. Part of me wondered if it was just more common than I thought and that everyone who was psychic thought they were a freak and tried to hide it. Another part of me wondered if maybe it was the universe's way of helping me learn to accept my abilities.

Emma came in the door just as my mom lit the first candle. She was my best friend, so there was no need for her to knock. She dropped her duffel bag and pulled me into a hug that sizzled with excitement.

"I know hosting a séance usually means bad news for someone," Emma said, "but it's so cool to be a part of it again."

I smiled. Her enthusiasm lifted my mood slightly. "I'm glad you're here."

Sophie and Diane shuffled around the house to shut the shades. We definitely didn't want anyone to see what we were up to. We still didn't know how the community would react if they found out the town's Halloween and herbal gurus had real powers.

I eyed Diane as she lowered the shade above the sink, and I wondered something out loud. "Do you think we'll ever tell people?"

"What?" my mom asked in confusion.

I pulled my eyes off Diane and looked at my mother. Drawing out a chair at the table, I sat down as I spoke. "I was just wondering what would happen if the community knew about us. Do you think they'd accept us?"

My mother shook her head in amusement. "Crystal,

I don't think you realize how lucky you are. We weren't lucky enough to have a network of psychics at our fingertips when we were growing up. My grandma was psychic, but that was it for me. Sophie did have a big family of psychics. But even so, we've all learned that not everyone is so accepting of the paranormal. I think it's best if the town went on believing Divination was based off the make believe. The ones who understand the true nature of some of our products will seek us out. Other people don't always understand."

I let her words sink in for a moment. Maybe I had been too lucky lately.

"Okay," I nodded and left it at that, but her words only made me wonder when the time would come for a friend to turn away from me because of my gift.

My mom flipped off the lights, and everyone situated themselves around the table. Emma and I had only been to one séance before, the one we held to contact Olivia Owen's ghost, which ended in me rescuing a classmate from an abusive relationship. Even though I was fairly inexperienced in séances, I was confident that if we could contact Melissa, I had the best team of people to do it sitting in my kitchen.

"Last time, we all held hands," I said, "so I think that's what we should do now." I gripped onto Emma's hand to my left and my mom's to my right.

"Remember, Crystal," my mom said, "this is your ghost, so you'll have to lead the séance."

I nodded. Even though I'd been doing my best over

the past few months to confront my abilities and get better at them, I wasn't entirely sure about doing this. *Is there another Sage out there I'm supposed to meet? Will Melissa make contact?*

I took a deep breath to calm my nerves. My mind told me to rush through this to get the answers that might save a girl's life, but I also knew that nothing would come if I hurried.

I spoke softly and gave a gentle reminder to everyone to clear their minds. I tried to let go of any uncertainties I had. When I met Melissa in the dressing room and she faded, it seemed like she wasn't coming back. Would a séance work, then? I didn't know.

I also couldn't help but notice that none of us knew anything about Melissa. All I knew was her face and her name. I didn't even have a last name. How could the rest of them focus on someone they couldn't even put a face to? Last time, we had something that belonged to the ghost: Olivia's volleyball jersey. This time, we had nothing.

Luckily, I'd practiced enough over the past few months that I was able to push these thoughts aside and clear my head. I opened my mind to the other side and encouraged everyone else to do the same. I could feel a heightened energy in the room, one that told me we were doing everything right, but I couldn't feel a spirit anywhere nearby.

"Melissa," I called out after a few minutes. I wished I had gotten her last name so I had more to go by. "You told me to help Sage. I need more answers. I need more so that I can help her."

We sat in silence for several long minutes. Nobody moved or spoke. We were all so concentrated on the spiritual realm that if someone was listening in on us, they wouldn't hear a thing. Even the breathing around the table had slowed to hardly make a sound.

"Melissa," I called out several minutes later. Nothing. Absolutely nothing.

Was it my uncertainty in this task that made it impossible? Was it because I had very little to go on to get her to come to me? All I could do was call her name.

So that's what I did. Another half hour must have passed. Every few minutes, I called Melissa's name. I periodically reminded everyone to clear their minds. Even with all the thoughts racing around in my own head, I felt confident in my connection with the other side. I knew I had cleared my mind enough that I should come up with *something*, but nothing happened.

After what must have been 45 minutes of silence, I finally broke the circle. "She's not going to show," I told everyone. Hadn't I already known that since she disappeared in the dressing room? I knew she wasn't coming back to help me, and that fact scared me, like I was all alone on this. Then I gazed around the table and remembered I wasn't alone.

"Even though Melissa probably isn't going to show up again, we can still save Sage," I told them with confidence. "We have until the wedding." A shiver traveled down my spine when I realized how little time that truly was.

4

I slumped to my bed in disappointment. "I can't let her die," I told Emma.

"Crystal, she's not going to die. She has you on her side." Emma sat next to me on my bed.

I gave a smile at her compliment, but I wasn't quite sure. In the past, it seemed like I'd never paid enough attention to my visions. This time, I wasn't going to make that mistake. Still, no one's life had depended on me before. Sure, I'd helped people who were in danger, but I'd never had to save someone from *death*.

The questions that sprang to my head only seemed to create a bigger problem. How was I going to prevent it? What could I do? How was she even going to die?

"I feel like I just wasted an hour. Trying to contact Melissa was useless, and now Sage is another hour closer to dying."

"Don't beat yourself up over it, Crystal," Emma said. "I have a good feeling about this. You're going to save her."

With Emma's practice, she'd become talented at assessing situations and determining if they were good or bad. At first, I didn't believe in her abilities, but I've started trusting them more and more. So when Emma said she had a good feeling about my involvement, it really did lift my spirits.

"I hope you're not lying to me," I told her, but I didn't think she was.

"Cross my heart and hope to die." Emma drew an imaginary X over her heart.

I paused for a moment and swallowed deeply. "You probably shouldn't say things like that."

She frowned. "Yeah, you're right. I'm sorry."

I stood from the bed and paced around the room to ease my nerves. "I don't want to waste any time trying to figure out how Sage is going to die and how I'm going to help her, but I don't know what else to do. I already tried to learn more about her online, but it's like she doesn't exist on the Internet. Don't you think that's weird?"

Emma nodded and shifted on the bed. "That is really weird. Doesn't she at least have a Facebook account?"

I shook my head. "Not that I could find. I'm wondering if the girl from the bridal shop is the same girl Melissa warned me about. I mean, why else would a ghost warn me about a girl named Sage if I was only going to meet a girl with that very same name minutes later? This doesn't make sense."

Before Emma could offer her opinion, my phone began buzzing in my pocket. "Hello?" I answered, sliding back down onto the bed.

"Crystal," Robin greeted.

Emma raised her eyebrows. "Is it Robin?" she whispered, leaning in until I could feel her breath on the side of my face.

I swatted her away but couldn't help but smile at Robin's voice despite the troubles I was having. "Yeah?"

"I just wanted to call and see how your thing went. Did you get everything figured out?"

"Not really," I answered honestly. "But I'm glad you called because I just remembered something. I was wondering when your next gig was. There's a girl I met today when we were shopping who said she wanted to check you guys out." I only hoped I wasn't wasting time on the wrong girl.

"We're playing this coming weekend at Bradshaw Park. I already told you about that. It's for Asher's brother's birthday party, remember?"

"Yeah, I guess I forgot that was this weekend. You don't mind if I invite someone?"

"Nah, Troy won't care if more people come. He'll probably just feel more popular or something."

"Thanks." I wanted to steer the conversation

toward Sage and her death so I could confide in Robin. To hell with him worrying. I knew if I wanted this relationship to last, I couldn't hide anything from him, not even things related to my abilities. "Um, about the girl I'm bringing. I have something to tell you about her."

"Uh, okay."

"When we were shopping for my dress, I saw this ghost." I paused to gauge his reaction.

Emma shifted on the bed and picked at her fingernails like she wasn't listening, even though I knew she was invested in every detail of the conversation.

"Okay," Robin said slowly as if he didn't know where I was going with this.

I stood again and paced a few steps around the room before flashing a glance at Emma, looking for some way to help explain it all. "She gave me a warning and told me a girl named Sage was going to die soon. I'm still not sure—"

"Wait," Robin interrupted. "Sage who?"

"Anderson. Well, that's what the ghost said."

"You're kidding."

"No, I'm not."

"You're telling me a ghost told you that Sage Anderson is going to die?"

"Yeah. What?" I paused for a second, and then realization sank in. "Do you know her?"

"She goes to my school. I mean, we're not exactly best friends, but she's my lab partner. Crystal, if Sage is going to die, we have to save her."

My knees rapidly grew weak. I sank back down onto the bed to steady myself.

"Crystal, what's wrong?" Emma asked.

I stuck a hand up to tell her to give me a minute. "Does the Sage you know work at Special Day Bridal?"

"I think so."

Suddenly, I became very excited. Perhaps the emotion was a bit unwarranted, but at least that meant the girl I met today was the girl I was supposed to save. Granted, she was in danger, but I wasn't completely lost and wondering whose death I could prevent.

"Robin," I said breathlessly into the receiver. "You're my connection!" I had been looking for something that would connect us earlier, and now Sage and I had something in common: Robin.

"What do you mean?" he asked.

"Are you at least close enough that she might hang out with you?"

I could practically hear Robin shrug on the other end of the line. "I guess so. She doesn't really hang out with anyone, but maybe if I asked her . . ."

I mentally added that bit of information to the weirdness surrounding Sage. I mean, it wasn't like she was socially awkward or super ugly or anything. How could she be a loner?

"You guys are practicing at Asher's on Tuesday night, right? What if you invited her to come watch you practice? Then Emma and I can come over, too." I was happy the end of basketball season a few weeks ago also marked the end of pep band for the school year, so I was finally free to watch them practice. "I don't think I can wait a whole week to learn more about her," I added.

"I guess I can try, but I don't know if she'll say yes."

"Thank you, Robin! Asher's parents won't mind?"

"No, they're pretty cool."

"Okay. Do you know much about Sage? I mean, does it seem like she's in danger?"

"Not that I've picked up on," he admitted. "We talk a little in class, but she mostly keeps to herself. I'll let you know if I notice anything, though."

"Thank you, Robin."

I hung up only for Emma to immediately jump into her inquisition. "What was that about? It sounded like he knows Sage? Did he say 'I love you?' Why didn't you say it back?"

I shoved her lightheartedly, mostly to hide the blush rising to my cheeks. "No, he didn't because neither of us have said it yet. It's not like you and Derek have, either."

"I'm waiting for him to say it first," she defended.

"Maybe I'm doing the same thing."

We both immediately dropped the subject because neither of us wanted to discuss the fact that even after five months, for both of our relationships, the "L" word still hadn't come up once.

"Anyway," I said, "Robin *does* know Sage. He's going to ask her to come to his practice on Tuesday."

"And I suppose you want me to drive you there," Emma said.

Emma had her driver's license, and I had only recently got my learner's permit. I nodded.

"Okay," she answered. "Derek's invited, too, right?"

"Yeah. As long as Asher's parents are okay with so many people coming along."

When I asked Mom about going to Asher's on Tuesday, she insisted I call to make sure his parents would be home. Mom was always more like a best friend to me than a mother, but ever since I started dating, she'd been getting more protective. The rule was that I couldn't hang out with Robin unless an adult was present or we were in public. I explained to her about Sage and her connection with Robin, and then she seemed more accepting of letting me go. She still made me call as a courtesy.

I wasn't exactly great friends with Asher yet, but we'd met a few months back after Robin and I started dating, so I had his number programmed into my phone. The good news was that Asher didn't care if we tagged along, and his mom was going to be there. Apparently, his family had this "the more, the merrier" policy.

I couldn't wait. That night, I lay in bed wide awake as Emma snored lightly on the fold-up cot next to me. I could usually get little bits of information about people just by focusing on them, but it never seemed to work when I was sent to save them. It's like the universe didn't think the little things were important when I knew fully well that they were.

I fell asleep without learning anything new about Sage Anderson.

5

I woke Sunday morning to Emma's ringtone. She shifted on the cot and reached for her phone in her overnight bag on the floor. The sunlight seeped through my curtains, casting a sliver of light across my bed. I checked my clock and found it was already 8:00. I stretched, thinking about how well I'd slept, and then the memory of everything that happened the day before came flooding back to me. Suddenly, I felt guilty for sleeping so well when a girl's life depended on me. But honestly, I had no idea what to do next.

"Derek wants us to hang out with him after he comes home from church," Emma told me.

What I really wanted to do was talk with Sage. I reached for my own phone on my nightstand and spun it around in my hands. I didn't even realize what I was doing until Emma spoke again.

"You're thinking about Sage, aren't you?"

"What?" I jerked my eyes up at her. How did she know?

"It's written all over your face. You're like an open book, Crystal."

I sighed. She was right about that.

"Be careful," Emma warned. "You don't want to come across too pushy. You want her to trust you."

I nodded and looked down in disappointment at my phone again. It felt like any moment I wasn't learning more about Sage was time wasted, but at the same time, I understood where Emma was coming from.

"So, Derek's?" I asked. "Sounds fun."

While we waited for Derek to get home, Emma insisted we have one of our psychic practice sessions. Normally we practiced after I was done babysitting Hope, but Emma said that since we'd be at Asher's later this week, doing it now would make up for our Tuesday practice.

With a reluctant eye roll, I agreed. She was right. Even with the progress we'd both made, I still needed to practice my abilities.

I unrolled my owl yoga mat across my carpet while Emma reached into her bag and pulled out her own mat. My room wasn't exactly the cleanest place on earth, but most of the mess was piled in front of my dresser where a heap of clean clothes sat unfolded and a drawer was open. That left enough room for the both of us to stretch out.

"How did you know?" I asked accusingly, eyeing Emma's yoga mat.

"What?" she asked innocently as she situated her mat on my floor.

"You were just using Tuesday as a convenient excuse, weren't you? You would have come up with anything to make us practice."

Emma shrugged as a smile crept across her lips. "You know me well."

I twisted my mouth up at her in discontent. Still, I couldn't help but be grateful for her persistence. Without it, I wasn't sure how good my abilities would be at this point. Plus, I was itching to make a psychic connection with Sage.

But, of course, I couldn't let Emma know I was happy about this practice session. There'd be too much pride in it for her.

"After our warm-up exercises, I thought we could practice more with your crystal ball," Emma said. "I mean, *you* should practice, but I'll be here to help if I can. I'm not nearly ready for crystal ball gazing yet."

I nodded. Maybe it would give me a glimpse into Sage's near future, like how she was going to die. Then I'd have a better idea of how I could save her. Unfortunately, I didn't have a way of controlling the information that came to me.

"Ready?" Emma asked, stretching her arms above

her head to loosen them up.

"Yep."

She fiddled with her phone for a few seconds until a soothing melody began playing out of it. Our first 10 to 15 minutes or so of each session was spent clearing our minds and relaxing our bodies. When we started these sessions, Emma would tell me what to do, but now we just gave each other time to do whatever our bodies felt was needed to clear our minds.

I took a few deep breaths and forced the muscles in my face to relax. I could hear Emma's deep breathing next to me. She let out a soft hum.

I breathed in and out slowly and deeply as I concentrated on different points in my shoulders and back to relieve any tension. The task proved difficult as I worried about my newfound responsibility toward Sage. *How can I save her when I don't know what danger she's really in?*

I rolled my head to the side to stretch my neck.

I tried my best not to think; I attempted to clear my mind, but it was to no avail. As time passed and I worked my way through my yoga poses, my thoughts ran in a web of connections that eventually took me to a memory of my father before he died.

I was all of four years old when our next door neighbor, Mrs. James, fell in her kitchen. In the winter, Dad was always there to shovel Mrs. James's driveway. In the summer, he'd even cut her grass without asking for anything in return. So when she fell and managed to reach a phone, my dad was the first person she called. He ran over to her house immediately and called an ambulance.

"Daddy," I remember asking, "why did you have to help Mrs. James? Why did she call you?" What I was really trying to ask is why she hadn't called the ambulance herself, but I don't think I ever quite worded it right because what my father said next stuck with me.

"Crystal," he had said, "sometimes we're called on to help other people. Sometimes it's because people trust us. Other times it's just sheer luck. And you know what? It's our duty to rise to the challenge and help them. If we don't help each other, that's when we stop being human."

I heard Emma shift on her mat, and I took this reminder to make my own body move. I folded my legs under me and positioned myself onto all fours, my head turned up and my belly sunk toward the floor in cow pose.

I wasn't entirely sure if I was remembering my father's words correctly, but as I looked back on them, I had to wonder if he was trying to tell me something more important than I ever imagined.

I pulled my chin and tailbone into my body and stretched my spine upward into cat pose.

Was he trying to tell me that someday I would be called on to help people? Because of my abilities?

Cow pose.

He knew my mom was psychic, so maybe he

thought I was, too, which turned out to be the truth.

Cat pose.

Was that why I was always so desperate to help anyone who crossed my path? Was it because of what my dad said to me when I was four?

I curled my toes into the mat, lifted my knees from the floor, and pushed my butt toward the sky to position myself into downward facing dog.

What would things be like if I hadn't been psychic like Mom had thought for so many years? No one would have come to me for help, and I wouldn't have a responsibility toward anyone.

I slowly lowered my entire body to the mat and then lifted my chest up into cobra pose.

A normal life. That sounded pretty nice. It'd be like it was before last Halloween.

I paused back in downward facing dog.

I'd be able to hang out with my friends care-free and enjoy my teenage years without abuse, abductions, and death on my mind.

I shifted my body weight between each of my legs, pressing my heels into the mat to stretch my calves.

But wait. That would mean that my mom would still be hiding her secret and that we wouldn't have this bond anymore. That would mean that Kelli might still be in an abusive relationship and that, after everyone but me gave up on her, Hope would still be in Lauren's hands. That would mean that Robin and I would have never taken that side trip last Thanksgiving and gotten to know each other and started dating.

That would mean that Sage wouldn't have a chance.

A loud clap snapped me out of my thoughts. I fell to my knees and jerked my eyes up toward the sound.

"I'm sorry," Emma said. "I didn't mean to clap that loud. Ready to move on?"

With me, Sage has a chance, I thought, which filled me with a sense of hope.

Emma and I continued through our exercises. We started by writing down three predictions for tomorrow. Mine were really dumb, like what was going to be on the lunch menu. We had done this exercise so many times that I could see little things like that with ease. What I really wanted was to see something about Sage, but even as I focused on her, I couldn't see even the tiniest bit of detail.

Next, Emma made me leave the room while she hid an object for me to find. I was gifted with psychometry like my mom. When I reentered the room, I knew exactly what she'd hidden before I even touched anything. That's because the one thing in the room that was always in its proper position was missing. Emma had hid my stuffed owl, Luna. I immediately unzipped Emma's duffel bag and found Luna sitting on top.

"Whoa." Emma took a step back in shock.

"What?" I asked with a shrug. "I didn't do anything different, did I?"

Emma nodded slowly, like she was unsure of what I'd just done. "You didn't even touch my hand to find out what was missing."

Oh. She was right. Normally I needed something to touch that had recently been around the hidden object.

"Well," I said, "I noticed Luna had moved as soon as I entered the room, so maybe since I already knew what was missing, I knew where it was."

"Or maybe you're just getting better," Emma theorized. "Or maybe it's because you're so attached to Luna."

"What?" I practically squeaked. "I am not."

That was such a lie, and Emma knew it. Still, I turned my face and put Luna back on her shelf so Emma wouldn't notice how blatantly I was lying—since my eyebrow twitched every time I lied. The truth was, I was attached to Luna. After all, my father had given her to me.

"Okay, your turn," I told Emma.

Emma didn't have psychometry. She could never tell what I hid, but she could get feelings about situations. It was like she could tell when she was hot or cold because of which decision felt better to her.

Once she left the room, I searched for something to hide. I couldn't make it too hard for her, but I also couldn't make it too easy. I stood in the middle of my room for several long moments wondering what I should hide for her. When my wandering eyes fell to my feet, I was reminded of the first time we played this game and Emma hid her sock. I decided to do the same. I slipped off the other sock just so she wouldn't notice I was missing one.

"Okay, you can come back in," I called.

She stood by my open door with her eyes closed for what seemed like forever. I knew she was trying to get "in the zone," as she put it, but her silence left me wondering if I had made it too hard for her. I sat on the end of my bed and simply observed.

After a while, she began moving around my room. She'd go one way and then turn around and pace a few steps the other way. She did this several times, inching closer and closer to the sock each time. Several long minutes passed. Finally, she stood over her duffel bag and opened her eyes.

"You hid it in the same place, you dirty little cheat!" she exclaimed.

"Well, I didn't think you'd look there."

She opened her bag and threw my sock at my face. We both laughed.

"Okay. Are you ready for crystal ball gazing?" Emma asked.

I sighed. "I guess." This was one thing I still wasn't good at, and it always made me nervous. I crossed the room and picked up my crystal ball from where it stood on my dresser. Every time I touched the ball, it called out to me somehow. Colors swirled in it, and I felt nothing but tranquility.

Suddenly, Emma's ringtone cut through the silence. I jumped, and the ball slipped out of my fingers. It fell with a thud onto the clothes in my open dresser drawer.

"I'm sorry!" Emma said. "It's just Derek. He says he's back from church."

"I guess our practice is cut a little short today." I knew that even as much as Emma loved practicing her psychic abilities, she wanted to get to her boyfriend's house as soon as possible.

"I guess so," she agreed.

I glanced back at my crystal ball and lazily decided to let it lay where it was. Besides, it looked kind of cozy tucked in a cradle made of my tees.

6

When we reached Derek's, we entered his house without knocking. I still found it weird, like I was intruding, but ever since Emma and Derek started dating, things had shifted slightly in our group of three. It wasn't so bad that I felt left out or like a third wheel or anything, but even after a few months, it was still awkward to witness their peck when they greeted each other. The good news was that Derek's parents adored Emma.

"Do you guys want to see it?" Derek asked excitedly.

"See what?" I replied.

"My driver's license. That's why I left school early on Friday. Remember? I texted you about it."

Derek handed over his license, and Emma and I

gazed at it with enthusiasm. Milo—Derek's dog—sniffed at me while I tried to get a good look, so I petted him softly to calm him down.

"That's great that you passed the first time, Derek," I said, momentarily reminding myself that now everyone I knew could drive and I was still the youngest one around. At least it gave me a chance to hang out with my friends when I needed a ride, though.

We said hello to his parents and twin sisters and then followed Derek to his bedroom—but had to leave the door open per his parents' rules. He eagerly told us about his driving test.

I sat in his desk chair while Emma and Derek claimed a seat on his bed.

"I know you haven't talked about it a lot, Derek," Emma started, "but this just reminds me of your birth parents. Did your mom and dad ever really tell you more about them?"

Derek had found out he was adopted when he got his learner's permit and he caught a glimpse of his birth certificate. When he finally admitted his secret—well, not so much admitted it as much as I found out because of my psychic abilities—he said he didn't care because his birth parents were dead and it didn't change that his adoptive parents were still his parents.

He shrugged in response to Emma's question. "I guess my mom and dad have always felt like my mom and dad. I don't really feel any need to search for information about my birth parents."

Emma ran her fingers through her curly dark hair. "Wouldn't it at least be nice to kind of know where you came from?"

"It's not like I'm having an identity crisis," Derek said lightheartedly, like he didn't care to know what happened to them. I couldn't bring myself to believe he wasn't at least curious.

"I know." Emma shifted on the bed. "I guess I just feel like if I found out I was adopted, I would at least do a Google search and try to figure out more about my birth parents."

Derek shrugged again. "I guess."

"Well, why not?" She stood from the bed and shooed me from my spot by Derek's computer. "What were their names?"

"Uh, Thomas and Sharon Woods. I got the Johnson last name from my mom and dad," he explained, meaning his adoptive parents.

Emma typed his dad's name into the search bar.

Meanwhile, I turned to Derek. "Want to hear about the crazy stuff that happened to me this weekend?"

"Psychic related?" he guessed.

I nodded.

Derek still had a hint of doubt about my abilities, but he'd been supportive about it the entire time. He said he wanted to believe it, and I found comfort in confiding in him. I told him about the warning and about meeting Sage at the bridal shop. I also told him about how I couldn't find anything online about Sage.

He agreed that her online absence was odd.

"Dang it," Emma complained, interrupting us. "Derek, why didn't your birth parents have less common names?" She didn't even look up when she said this, which led me to believe it was a rhetorical question.

"Anyway," I continued, "Robin knows Sage and is going to try to get her to come watch his band practice on Tuesday. Emma is driving me, and you're invited, too."

"I bet Emma is dying to go," he teased. "She drools over musicians."

I laughed because it was so true, but Emma remained glued to the screen like she didn't hear us. Derek wasn't in the school band like Emma and I were, but he had conveniently began learning guitar since they started dating.

I caught a glimpse of the guitar in the corner of his room and raised my eyebrows. "You know, you don't need to learn guitar for Emma to drool over you. That just comes naturally to her."

He tried to hide it, but I could see him blushing. "I'm not learning for her," he lied.

"Yeah, right," I teased.

"This is useless." Emma swiveled the chair back toward us. "There are too many people named Thomas and Sharon Woods in the world."

"Emma, you've only been looking for a few minutes," I pointed out.

"It's fine," Derek said. "I'll search more information about them later if it means that much to you. Who wants to play Xbox?"

7

Monday couldn't pass by any slower. I did my best to focus my energy on Sage when I had a spare moment, but the little things still wouldn't come to me. I wasn't sure if it was because I was so anxious waiting in anticipation for Tuesday night or if that was just the way the universe worked. I was 99 percent sure it was a combination of both.

At lunch, Robin texted me. *Sage said yes! See you tomorrow.*

That's great! I texted back, which lifted my mood.

I still have a few weeks left, I reminded myself.

After school, I picked up Hope from the elementary school and walked her home. We played games for a couple of hours until her mom came home from work. Hope was a surprisingly smart and insightful first grader. Since I'd found her after she'd been abducted last year, she knew I was psychic. I almost considered telling her about Sage because I felt, despite her young age, she would understand.

But I didn't tell her. Her dad had died last year, and I really didn't want to bring up the topic of death. Although that was something we had in common—that both of our dads died—I did my best to avoid the subject, and Hope never brought it up, either.

I arrived home just in time for supper. I took my seat at the table after greeting my mom and Teddy.

"Your mom says something happened on Saturday, Kiddo," Teddy told me once we started eating. "She said you might want to tell me yourself and that I might be able to help."

"That would be great!"

Teddy was a police officer, so whatever danger Sage was in, he might be able to find out what that was. I didn't mention that I wished I could find that out myself through my abilities, but having the answer through Teddy was better than no answer at all.

I immediately delved into the story of what happened with Melissa's warning, and I even told him how I couldn't find anything about Sage online. By the time I was done, my first bite of lasagna was lukewarm.

"Hmm . . ." Teddy mused. "It is really weird that she isn't online. These days, teens post so much that it's easy to bust them for drug abuse and things like that."

"I know. Weird, right? Do you think you can find

anything out about her?"

"I'm technically not supposed to access police records for things like this, but I will look into it. Anderson, right?"

"Yep." I turned to my mother. "No one else has seen anything that can help?"

She shook her head as she bit into her food. "Sorry, sweetie. If I could give her a reading, see her in person, maybe . . ."

"That's actually a really good idea," I admitted, "but I hardly know her. I can't just text her and be like, 'Hey, my mom wants to read your future. Can you come over?'"

Mom and Teddy laughed, but I didn't think it was that funny. Just then, the front door opened, and I watched Emma enter the living room.

"I'll just be a minute, Emma," I told her as she came farther into the house. I shoveled my lasagna into my mouth and chugged my milk.

"Do you want some food?" Teddy asked.

He was a great cook, so it was tough to refuse dinner from him, but Emma politely declined and told him she already ate.

Emma and I escaped to my room for our psychic practice. We started with our normal yoga routine and then wrote down a few predictions. So far, I hadn't missed one in over a month, but it was still only little things like what the gas price would be tomorrow. I didn't consider many of these predictions accomplishments, although I congratulated Emma on each one she got right. She only had about a 15 percent success rate, so it meant a lot more to her when she was accurate.

"Maybe you could predict how Derek's birth parents died," Emma suggested.

I wasn't sure that was something I could just *see*. "I don't know, but I can try. Honestly, though, I doubt I'll see anything about that. Why are you so interested anyway?"

Emma's eyes darted down to the paper in her hand, and she nervously pushed dark curls out of her face without meeting my eyes. "I'm not that interested. I was just curious."

Normally, Emma wasn't such a bad liar. I eyed her, wondering where her curiosity was coming from. After a few moments of silence, I realized what it was. I didn't have to be psychic to figure it out; I simply knew Emma well. Her parents had just finalized their divorce. She was either using Derek's birth parents' issue as a distraction from that, or she was looking for reassurance that her own family matters weren't that bad. It was probably a combination of both.

I turned back to my piece of paper and closed my eyes to clear my mind. Sometimes I knew what I was writing. Other times, my subconscious took over and I didn't even realize I was making predictions. That's what it was like now, and although I wasn't completely aware of it, I knew that something was different about this time. My mind cleared so much that I wasn't even aware of my surroundings. It was like I was lost in a different dimension where tranquility ruled the world.

Slowly, the hum of my laptop and the noises of the TV in the living room came back to life. I blinked a few times until my room focused, and then I gazed down at my sheet of paper. The handwriting was crooked as usual, but something about the prediction riled me. I had no idea what to make of it.

Tomorrow you will find the answers to the questions you never asked. Be prepared to listen carefully.

"Great," I complained to Emma, who was already watching me expectantly from her spot next to my desk. "I got another fortune cookie prediction."

"What does it say?" she asked with a hint of excitement in her voice.

I handed her my sheet of paper. "How do I know what questions are being answered if I haven't asked them yet?"

Emma pressed her lips together. "At least you finally have something about Sage."

"What do you mean?" I asked as she handed the sheet of paper back.

"Well, it says 'tomorrow.' Tomorrow is the day we're going to meet Sage so you can learn more about her. It must be about her, right? I mean, it only makes sense."

She had a point, but I wasn't entirely convinced.

8

Emma picked me up straight from Hope's house on Tuesday. I climbed in the back seat behind Derek, and we all rode to Asher's together. I silently stared out the window at the passing scenery, which was still recovering from the last snow we had and was slowly turning green. Emma and Derek were talking in the front seat, and she was asking him about his birth parents again. Derek said he didn't find anything online and was going to ask his adoptive parents more about them if it meant that much to Emma. Something in his tone told me he didn't like poking into this mystery, but Emma didn't seem to notice his reluctance.

Later, they were discussing Emma's extensive music collection while the radio played in the background, but I was so nervous about meeting Sage again that I didn't say much.

When we made it to Asher's house, his mom told us everyone else was already in the basement, which she kindly explained was soundproofed as not to disturb the neighbors. They weren't playing yet, and there were a few other people I didn't know gathered around to listen. Sage wasn't there, which made my palms sweat nervously. Would she make it? Or was this night wasted?

When I spotted Robin, I knew that even if Sage didn't show, coming here wasn't for nothing. I fell into his arms immediately. It'd been over two weeks since we'd seen each other, and I missed him terribly. He placed a soft kiss on my lips, which earned us a few whistles from his band members. Robin grabbed a pillow from the couch and threw it at Tyler, who played the drums.

He introduced Emma and Derek to his band members. There was Tyler on percussion, Logan on keyboard, Skip on bass guitar, and Asher on lead guitar. Robin, of course, sang lead vocals.

Asher introduced us to the other people in the room, including Troy—Asher's younger brother—Troy's girlfriend Faith, and Faith's brother Andrew.

"Well, we're going to get started soon," Robin announced. "I will warn you that it's going to get kind of loud. Feel free to take a seat. Oh, and there's some pop upstairs in the fridge if anyone wants some." Robin left a kiss on the top of my head before turning to situate his microphone.

Luckily, there were two huge couches set up in the basement, so there was enough room for all of us. Asher strummed a few chords on his guitar, and then he adjusted his amp volume. Everyone else tinkered around and did the same thing with their instruments.

Movement by the stairs caught my eye. My heart fluttered excitedly at the sight of auburn hair. It hung loose around Sage's body, and she tucked a strand of it behind her ear while scanning the room uncertainly. My first opportunity to learn more about Sage had finally arrived.

"Sage," Robin greeted, heading over to her. "I'm glad you could make it. Let me introduce you to everyone."

As Robin started the second round of introductions, Sage's eyes fell on me. They widened a bit in surprise and recognition. I smiled back as friendly as I could. After Robin finished introducing everyone, Sage finally made her way over to me.

"That band you were talking about . . . It's them?"

"Yep," I answered proudly.

"Which one is your boyfriend?"

"Robin."

"Good choice." Almost immediately, a blush rose to her cheeks. "I didn't mean it like that. I don't like him like that. I just mean he's a good guy."

I gave a lighthearted laugh in hopes of making her feel better, but it was tough to force a laugh when I was face-to-face with a girl I knew was going to die soon. "Yeah, he is. Do you need somewhere to sit?" I offered her the spot next to me, and she sat down.

The band started playing, and I listened the best I could, but my mind was so overcome with worries about Sage that the blaring noise from the amps seemed almost nonexistent. How was I going to work up the courage to talk to her? And how could I talk to her over the music?

Robin stopped the band and had them rework the verse they were on.

I turned to Sage. "They're pretty good, right?"

She nodded.

How was I going to get through to her? I had to know what type of danger she was in, yet I knew I couldn't just blurt it out.

"Do you want a pop?" I asked over the music.

"What?" Sage shouted back.

"Do you want a pop?" I repeated. I gestured for her to follow me. When we entered the kitchen, the music from downstairs was surprisingly faint. "Robin said there was pop in the fridge if we wanted some."

"Hi, girls." Asher's mom greeted us as she entered the kitchen. "I'm making cookies, and they'll be done in a few minutes. You can grab a soda out of the fridge if you want one."

"Thank you." I opened the door to the refrigerator, which was huge compared to mine. There had to be a dozen different types of drinks. I grabbed a Sprite for myself.

"How was the rest of your weekend?" I asked Sage as she grabbed a diet Mountain Dew. "I mean, after my mom and her crazy wedding party left the bridal shop."

She laughed lightheartedly. "If you think you guys are crazy, you should see the groups that come in there. Compared to some, your wedding party is pretty normal."

If only she knew . . .

Sage slid into one of the chairs around the kitchen table and opened her pop can. I pulled out a seat next to her.

"You know, you should come again, to Robin's band practice, I mean." As soon as I said it, I realized my invitation sounded a bit premature since the practice had barely started, but I couldn't think of anything else to say.

Sage smiled at me. "Yeah, I think I might. It was really sweet of him to invite me. Not a lot of people are so nice, especially entering a new school as a senior. Most people already have their group of friends and don't want to hang out with the new girl."

"I didn't realize you were new here. Where are you from?"

She stared down at her can. "Oh, uh, I'm from . . . around. It's just a new school."

Her tone told me that it wasn't something she wanted to talk about, so I didn't push it, but I did make a mental note to figure out where she lived before she moved to the city and why she moved. Something about it felt important to me.

I did my best to keep her talking. "Robin says the band is looking to add a female voice to the group. Is that something you might be interested in?"

She shook her head lightly. "I'd rather not be in front of big crowds."

I nodded in understanding. I wasn't thrilled about being in front of crowds, either, unless I was playing a solo on my clarinet in band. "You never even played in front of crowds when you played an instrument?" I remembered her telling me she used to play, but I couldn't recall the details.

"Oh, I did. I just . . . don't anymore."

"What did you play?"

She set her Mountain Dew down on the table and tugged at her long sleeves. "Saxophone. It was good for a while, but I had to give it up. So, how did you and Robin meet?"

She was obviously trying to change the subject, and as much as I wanted to know whatever secrets she was hiding, I definitely didn't want to push it and risk my chance at her trusting me. I knew I didn't have a lot of time with her, but I also understood that patience was a virtue.

I told Sage about how Robin and I met because his uncle was getting married to my mom. The whole time, questions raced through my head. *What can I say to pinpoint what type of danger Sage is in? I can see that she's trying to hide something from me, but what is it?*

I remembered my prediction from the day before and wondered what I was supposed to be listening for. It sounded like Sage was hiding something, but nothing she'd said seemed very significant, except for maybe that she transferred schools. Did something bad happen at her last one that she had to leave? What if there was someone dangerous at her last school?

"Your mom doesn't think that's weird?" Sage asked about Robin and me.

"No, everyone is pretty cool with it."

"Well, I guess. You're not blood related."

A stillness settled over the room as we both struggled to come up with something to say. Sage finally broke the silence. "Do you want to go back down and listen to them again?"

I honestly didn't want to. I wanted to learn more about her and the danger she was in, but telling her she was going to die would only make me look crazy. If only I was better at being subtle.

I followed Sage down the stairs and took my spot back on the couch, but sadly, I didn't get another chance to talk with her privately.

After Echo Score finished practicing, Robin and I finally had a moment alone. Sage had already gone home, which left me a little disappointed, but I was happy to have a second with Robin. Everyone was finishing up the cookies in the kitchen when he pulled me aside into the hallway that led to the bedrooms.

He wrapped his arms around my waist and pressed his lips gently to mine. For a moment, I completely forgot about Sage, as if Robin had some power that could magically melt all my troubles away.

He drew away from me and smiled. "So, how'd it go with Sage? Anything?"

I shook my head in disappointment. "I wish I could say there was."

Robin held me close to his chest, and I wrapped my arms around his body for comfort. "It will work out," he assured me. "I've seen you save people before. You're the kind of girl who can't *not* save someone when they're in trouble."

"So, I'm, like, the opposite of a damsel in distress?"

Robin laughed. "I guess you could say that."

I buried my face in his chest and inhaled his fresh spring scent. It made everything seem okay for a few seconds until I pulled away and Sage's face flashed through my mind. How could I be enjoying myself when she was going to die soon and I was the only one who could do anything about it? It didn't seem fair.

"Come on, Crystal," Robin insisted. "I hate to see you like this. Things are going to work out. We'll figure this out together, okay?"

I shyly met his gaze. How could he know that for certain?

He didn't say another word but instead pulled me close again and crushed his lips to mine. That gave me reassurance even after we parted. After all, I still had a few weeks to save her.

On the way home, I relayed everything Sage had said back to my friends in hopes that they'd help me make sense of it all. The whole time, I wondered if there was anything significant in her words, but nothing jumped out at me except for her transferring schools. Was that the piece of information I needed to solve this mystery?

When I arrived home, I slumped to bed and fell asleep almost instantly. I only hoped my dreams would give me something good.

9

That night, I dreamt about death.

A red sedan drove through the thick rain. The tires sprayed water up as the car pushed through puddles that gathered on the road and ran down into the ditch. A bright glow filled the scene as if it was still daytime, but the clouds were so thick, and the rain was coming down so hard that visibility was near non-existent.

The car approached another corner, and before I knew what was happening, it hydroplaned until one of its wheels slipped into the ditch. The car's gathered momentum sent it off the road and down the slight dip neighboring it.

My heart beat wildly in my chest. I wanted to scream for the people in the car, to give some sort of warning, but I already knew it was too late for them.

The vehicle flipped twice before it landed on its top, its wheels spinning toward the sky.

***

I woke with a start and found myself lying in a puddle of my own sweat. I knew it was a vision of some sort, but what did it mean? Someone had died. But who?

I thought about it for several long moments before it hit me. Of course! Derek's birth parents. Emma had asked me to figure out how they died, and now I knew.

That Wednesday morning, Emma and I walked to school together like normal. I didn't think it was fair to tell her about Derek's parents before I told Derek what I had seen, so I kept quiet, intending to tell them both about my dream later. Emma and I entered the doors to the school a little early.

It was typical of Derek to get to school just in time for the first period warning bell, so I wasn't worried until I heard him call out my name just as I reached my locker.

"Crystal!" Derek rushed up to me. He seemed out of breath.

"Are you okay?" I asked.

Emma's eyes widened in surprise a few lockers down from mine. She immediately pushed through the crowd of students on their way to their own lockers.

Derek nodded and then sucked in another long breath.

"Were you running?" I asked. I tried to stay calm,

but my palms began sweating. What had happened? Was he okay?

"Derek, what's wrong?" Emma put a gentle hand on his shoulder, but he didn't tear his gaze from me.

"Last night when I got home, I did a little more digging on my birth parents. I tried out a whole bunch of different key terms, like the city I was born in and stuff like that. I asked my mom about it. At first, she wouldn't tell me anything, but then she told me she thought my birth dad was an accountant and my birth mom was a nurse, so I used those search terms, too. Anyway, I kind of went crazy with keywords and eventually found all this information on them."

"Do you know how your parents died?" Emma asked the same time I breathed a sigh of relief knowing that he was okay.

"It was a car crash, wasn't it?" I guessed. "They died in the rain."

Emma and Derek both stared at me wide eyed.

"No, but how did you—?" Derek started. "Hold on. I'll get to that in a minute. This morning, I was thinking about what you said about Sage not being online. So, I thought I could do the same thing with her, you know, narrow the search a little bit. Anyway, I remember what you said about her playing saxophone. I found this."

Derek handed me a printout image of a paused video. In it, Sage was standing on a stage in the center of a concert band with her saxophone to her lips. Everyone else was sitting down, most of them hidden behind the stands. The director was facing directly at her. It was clear she was playing a solo.

If she was good enough to play solos, why did she quit? I wondered. I didn't say anything; I simply studied the image, amazed that Derek actually found something on her. *And why did she tell me she didn't like being in front of crowds? This photograph proves otherwise.*

"I can show you the video later. She's *really* good. But that's not all."

I tore my gaze from the photo and looked back up at Derek. What else had he found?

"What you said about the car crash in the rain . . ." Derek paused for a moment. "It wasn't my parents. It was Sage's."

I drew in a sharp breath. Part of me was surprised that I'd seen something related to Sage. Another part of me was shocked that Derek had dug up this information. The biggest part of me, however, was stunned to hear that Sage was an orphan. I could only partially relate because my dad had died, but I couldn't imagine losing both of my parents.

He handed me a news article, and all I could do was stare dumbfounded at it. Emma peeked over my shoulder.

"How did you find this?" I asked him in amazement.

"See, that's the funny thing. I was trying out this search term that I thought wasn't going to go anywhere. I just did it on a whim, and then this came up."

"What was the search term?" Emma asked.

My mouth went dry, and I tried to swallow, but I couldn't. As my eyes scanned the news article, I already knew what term he'd searched.

"Well, Crystal said the ghost's name was Melissa. I searched for Sage and Melissa Anderson and found the article about Melissa's death."

***

I spent all of first period reading and rereading the article about how Melissa and her parents died. It said that the family was driving to their daughter's concert performance. It was last summer, so I figured she was part of a traveling music group or maybe she went to band camp like I had a few summers back. The article didn't say. It didn't actually name Sage because she was still a minor, but some people who knew the family had left comments with her name in it.

Now I knew why she had stopped playing. Now I knew who Melissa really was.

But questions still nagged at me. What does that mean for Sage's death? How was she in danger? How could I save her?

I wanted to hurl when I realized that I only had three and a half weeks to figure it out.

10

Anticipation taunted me as I waited to talk with Teddy about what he found out about Sage, if he found out anything. With school, babysitting, and Robin's band practice, I hadn't had a chance to talk with Teddy since Monday night. I was so out of it at Hope's house that she won every game of checkers we played.

She eventually noticed my mood and asked me what was wrong.

"It's just . . . teenage stuff," I told her. I knew Hope was smart for her age and had an idea about my abilities, but I still wasn't completely open to telling her about Sage.

"Boyfriend troubles?" she asked in the most casual tone that I laughed out loud at her. What would a seven-year-old know about boyfriend troubles?

"How about we watch a movie?" She kindly placed her hand on mine for comfort.

I smiled. "Sounds great."

Hope's mom returned home the same time the movie ended. I said goodbye and walked back to my own house at a quicker pace than normal. When I reached home, I immediately rushed to the kitchen where I knew Teddy was already preparing supper.

"Did you find out anything?" I blurted.

"You mean about Sage?" Teddy asked, turning to the sink to fill a pot of water.

"I can't help but worry about her," I admitted.

"I did find a few things out."

"Well?" I asked expectantly.

He paused, shutting off the water. Something in his demeanor made me suspect he was reluctant to tell me what he knew. "Her parents died," he said with a hint of sorrow to his voice.

"I know. A car accident."

Teddy's eyes locked on mine, and he looked momentarily shocked. Then, as if he remembered I was psychic, he relaxed a little bit. "She's living with her aunt and uncle on her mom's side."

Okay, so the switching schools thing was starting to come together, but something in Teddy's tone told me there was more.

"What else?" I gripped onto my owl necklace, hoping the news wouldn't be all bad.

Just then, my mom entered the kitchen. I glanced at

her and then back at Teddy.

"Come on, Teddy," I insisted. "You can tell me anything. I swear I can handle it."

He leaned up against the counter and took a deep breath. He exchanged a glance with my mom like he wasn't sure if he should tell me or not.

"Just tell me," I demanded with almost too much volume.

Teddy set his pot on the stove and shoved his hands in his pockets but didn't meet my eyes. "Sage's paternal uncle has been missing for the last five years," he finally said.

Silence filled the kitchen for a few moments as I absorbed this information.

"Okay. How does that put her in danger?" I asked.

"There's a warrant out for his arrest."

"So, he's on the run from something. Is Sage in danger from him?"

Teddy shrugged. "It's possible, but I doubt it."

"Why? What did he do?" I felt my mom's hands touch my shoulders for comfort, but I was too annoyed at how Teddy was beating around the bush. I shook her off. "Teddy, just tell me. I have to protect her."

He took a long breath before finally answering. "Child abuse. He's wanted for abusing Sage, and I don't mean hitting her and stuff. It was a lot worse than that."

My breath caught, and I stared at Teddy in horror. How could someone do that to a little girl? How could that happen to someone I knew?

I balled my hands into fists. "Anything else?"

He shook his head.

"Then I'm not hungry." I turned and raced to my bedroom.

I fell down on my bed and buried my head in my pillow. I hoped it would help stifle the lump forming in my throat. My face grew hot, and I squeezed my eyes shut as if that would help my problems go away. I didn't want to imagine what Sage had been through, and I was terrified of what I had just been put up against.

If all I had to do was prevent Sage from getting in a car that would cause a death like her family's, that would be simple. There wouldn't be anyone working against me. But instead of saving Sage from a car crash or some natural accident, I had to save her from someone dangerous.

But what if her uncle is irrelevant? I wondered. *What if it is a car crash or something like that that's going to kill her? I need to find some way to be certain before I start jumping to conclusions.*

A knock rapped at my door.

"Crystal," my mom called, "can I come in?"

I forced down the lump in my throat and sat up in my bed. "Yeah. Come in."

My mom took a seat next to me. "Sweetie, I know that kind of information is tough to swallow."

You have no idea, I thought as the lump in my throat began rising again.

"It's harder when you know the person," she

continued. "But look, sweetie. We're going to figure this out." She ran a hand through my hair like she always did to comfort me. "Have your abilities ever failed you before?"

I didn't meet her gaze, but I did put some real thought into her question, and she was right. They hadn't. But I hadn't even been using them for a year. Surely I was bound to make a mistake at some point.

"That doesn't mean they won't fail me this time," I told her.

"Why would they when you're so determined to help her?"

"Maybe I'm too determined," I said a little too aggressively. I took a breath and adjusted my tone. "I mean, I'm so focused on Sage that I don't actually see anything about her. The only thing I've seen is the car crash that killed her parents."

"Remember when you had this same problem with Hope?" my mom asked.

I nodded.

"Remember how spending time with Robin helped you get your mind off things and you started seeing more?"

I nodded again.

"Maybe that's what you need to do, then. You need to get your mind off Sage first."

"Easier said than done."

"You could spend some time with your friends this weekend to try clearing your mind," she suggested.

"I guess Robin and I could do a double date with Emma and Derek." I shrugged. "I don't know. That just makes me feel like I'm abandoning Sage or something." But if it was the only way I would get the answers I needed . . . I had to know what danger she was in. How else was I going to prevent her death?

"Sweetie, you won't be abandoning her. The point is to make progress."

"I know." I stared down at my hands.

"Hey," my mom said, forcing me to look at her. "You're not the only one who cares about Sage. None of us want to see her get hurt. I may not be able to use my abilities to help her, but I will do whatever I can to make sure your abilities do. I'm not going to just leave you hanging, okay?"

I nodded.

A silence stretched between us for several long seconds. "Mom," I finally said. "You told me once that you had to save someone's life. How did you handle it?"

My mom shifted on my bed and inched closer to me. "I guess I never told you about that, huh? Did I ever tell you anything about how Teddy and I met?"

"Mom, don't change the subject."

Her eyes bore into mine seriously.

I blinked a few times before finally realizing what she was saying. "No!" I practically shouted in surprise. "You don't mean—Teddy was going to die?"

My mom nodded, but a smile played at the corner of her lips like she was proud of saving him.

"How?" My voice came out in almost a whisper this time. All she'd ever told me before was that they met while she was out on a walk. There was never anything paranormal about the story as far as I knew.

"It was right around the time he got the job on the force here in Peyton Springs. I kept dreaming about his face, only I'd never met him. I didn't even know his name, so I had no idea how I was going to save him."

Her expression fell, and she stared at a spot on the floor like she was remembering something horrible. "I kept watching him die night after night, and I was sure there wasn't anything I could do about it. I didn't know when he was going to die. I couldn't pinpoint the place in my dream. I didn't even know who he was."

"What happened?" I leaned in closer, engrossed in her story.

"You'd think being a police officer, Teddy would have been in danger while on duty. It wasn't that at all. In my dream, I kept seeing this big brown dog chase this orange tabby cat. I'd watch them tear through the streets until the cat raced underneath a ladder. Each night, the dog followed the cat underneath the ladder, and each night, he'd send it off balance. Every night, Teddy was at the top of that ladder. Every night, he fell. In my dreams, he always died. He was supposed to break his neck."

"How did you save him if you didn't know how?"

"It's funny how the universe works. Earlier that day, one of our clients called and put in an order for some herbs and candles – the kind we use for contacting spirits and things like that. She called later and said that she was sorry, but she wouldn't be able to make it to pick them up. She said she'd come another day, but I offered to drop them off. It was on the other side of town, but you were staying over at Emma's that night, so I didn't mind walking over there."

My mother paused for a moment to take a breath. "After I dropped off her order, I was walking back home, and I saw this orange tabby cat come tearing down the street. I knew . . . I just knew it was the same one I saw in my dreams. I didn't even think about it. I ran after the cat, but I wasn't as quick as it was, and just as I started following it, the brown dog appeared. I kept running.

"As they disappeared around the side of a building, I caught a glimpse of the ladder in my peripheral vision. The cat and dog were still weaving through the streets. In a split second, I decided to head to the ladder, hoping to cut them off."

She shook her head but smiled in humor. "Teddy didn't even realize I was there. I gripped onto the ladder just as the cat and dog were coming around that side of the building. That's the first time Teddy looked down and noticed me there. The dog managed to hit the ladder the same way it always had when I saw it in my dreams, but since I was holding on, it didn't knock it off balance."

"Seriously?" I asked. "That's how you two met?"

She nodded.

"It sounds more like you made that up," I said with a small laugh.

"It's true!" she defended, but it was clear she didn't think I was serious. "I had a tough time explaining why I was holding onto his ladder, but he even joked that if I wasn't there, he may have broken his neck. Of course, I couldn't tell him how right he was about that. And how could I? He was up there cleaning the gutters for his elderly landlord just because he's nice like that. You don't tell someone that a good deed is going to kill them."

"Have you ever told him he was going to die that day?" I was partially curious because it was my mom and Teddy, but I was also nervous about the answer. What if I had to tell Sage one day about her pending death? How would she handle it? How would *I* handle it, for that matter?

"I didn't even think to explicitly tell him," my mom admitted. "I don't think about it a lot, but I'm sure he's figured it out." She ran her fingers through my hair again. "But you see what I mean? You wouldn't get these warnings and visions if the universe thought you couldn't do something about them. It works in funny ways, but it manages to *work*."

I nodded in understanding. Part of me believed her wholeheartedly, but part of me still worried. "What exactly is the universe? The 'other side,' I mean. Why do we have these visions? Are they all from spirits and things like that?"

"That's something that has always been a mystery to all of us. Most of us believe it's our ancestors and other spirits who are able to see these things and then communicate with us from the other side."

"And what do you believe?"

"Honestly? I think a lot of it has to do with the universe making things right. I think there are times when cause and effect get out of control, and we're sent to balance it out. I'm not sure if all our visions come from spirits, but I definitely won't argue that there are spirits on the other side helping us out."

"How is it that we've never had this conversation?" I asked with a small laugh.

My mom looked at me seriously for a moment, and then she broke the silence. "Because I don't want to tell you what to believe. How can I put that on you when I'm not entirely sure myself?"

I blinked a few times as I absorbed her words. "I guess I never thought about it enough to decide what's worth believing in. After all these months, I still don't know how it all works."

"I'm sorry."

"For what?"

"That I can't explain to you how it all works. I know I'm your mom and I'm supposed to know everything, but I don't. I shouldn't be admitting this to you, but your abilities intimidate me a little bit."

My gaze flew to hers in shock.

"I mean, at first I thought I had so much I could teach you, but now after everything that's happened, I think you have more to teach *me*. Your abilities are truly amazing, Crystal. I've tried to teach you what I know about it all, but I don't know how much more I can help, especially when you're so reluctant to learn."

I twisted my face at her. "What's that supposed to mean?" The words didn't come out spiteful, but I was a little offended by her statement. I'd been working hard to practice my abilities.

"You have this 'let's get it over with' attitude. If you'd just relax and welcome your abilities with open arms, it may not be as difficult for you."

Now I was starting to get upset. What was with her picking on me like this? "I am trying!" I defended.

"I'm sorry, sweetie. I didn't mean to offend you. I'm only trying to help."

"I know, but it's tough to hear something like that when I'm already trying so hard."

"I'm sorry." My mom pulled me close into an embrace. "Let me know if you need any more help, okay?"

Then my mom left the room.

11

Just as my mom's footsteps faded down the hall, I heard Emma's coming toward my room. I quickly took a breath to compose myself; I didn't want my mood over my mother's accusations to show. I stole a quick glance in my mirror and put on a smile.

A second later, Emma burst into my room. "I am *so* sorry I'm late."

"Late?" I glanced at my clock. She was only a few minutes later than normal, and it's not like our practice sessions were set in stone. "It's fine, Emma," I assured her, and I really meant it. If she had come earlier, my mom and I wouldn't have finished our conversation. Sure, I was hurt that my mom felt I wasn't trying with my abilities, but I was also glad she told me the story about Teddy and opened up to me about her opinions.

"Derek and I lost track of time," Emma started.

"Seriously, Emma," I cut her off, "it's okay. You can be late for our psychic sessions. They don't have to start on the dot." I smiled at her teasingly.

Emma placed a hand on her hip and narrowed her eyes at me. "You just want to get out of it, don't you?"

I knew she was just poking fun at me, but I couldn't help but realize how much truth there was to her words. She was right, and my mom was, too. I was always reluctant to practice, and I wasn't doing my best to understand my abilities.

I sighed and rose from my bed. I didn't know what else to do, so I began arranging a few things on my desk. "Actually, not tonight. I do want to practice." I didn't let my gaze meet Emma's. Something about admitting this felt so out of character to me that I was afraid of what Emma would think. But she didn't say anything.

I broke the silence. "Dinner won't be ready for a while. Do you want to maybe do some research until it's done?"

"Research?" she asked with surprise. "Since when are you into research?"

I shrugged, but her words cut at my heart a little. "I just thought it'd be a good way to kill time." I turned away from her and reached for my phone on my bedside table so she wouldn't see my expression. Emma could read me like a book, and I knew there was self-doubt written all over my face. If she noticed, though, she didn't mention it.

"What do you want to research?" she asked as she took a seat on my bed.

"I don't know, actually." I set my phone back down—there wasn't anything on it to check—and took a seat next to her. "Is there anything fun you've come across lately?"

"Oh, there are tons of fun things." Her eyes brightened. "I try to focus my research on your abilities, but there are other things we can learn about."

"Like what?"

"There are things like astrology and tarot card reading we haven't really looked into, but I know you aren't really interested in all that."

She was right. I wasn't terribly interested, but who's to say I couldn't give it a shot? After all, my mom was a great tarot card reader.

"And there are things like telekinesis," she continued.

"You think that's a real thing?" I asked skeptically.

Emma shrugged. "It's not really any more unbelievable than seeing the future, is it?"

I stared at her for a minute because I wasn't sure if it was. I also wasn't sure if she was looking for a real answer.

"We could also research astral travel," she suggested.

"That's, like, seeing things outside your body, right?"

She nodded excitedly. "Yeah. It's like an out of

body experience. It's where your spirit leaves your body and travels on the astral plane."

"That one sounds interesting," I admitted, "even though I don't have that ability."

"Maybe it's something you can achieve, kind of like how I've been learning to be psychic but wasn't born with it."

I nodded, although I wasn't sure if I would be leaving my body any time soon. "Okay," I agreed. "Let's do some research on that one, then."

Emma and I read about astral travel for a while until she reminded me to look up the video of Sage playing the saxophone. I pulled out the sheet of paper Derek had given me earlier and used that to quickly find it through an Internet search. Emma and I sat silently as we listened to the crisp tone and melodic tune coming from Sage's saxophone.

Emma's mouth hung open in shock. "Wow. She's really talented."

I nodded in agreement. "I know. It's sad that she doesn't play anymore."

"There's no one in our band who can play that well."

"Except maybe a first chair clarinet player," I teased, but then I realized how insensitive that suggestion was. No way could I ever compete with Sage's talent. I quietly turned back to the screen.

"Why do you think she stopped playing?" Emma asked.

"The article on her parents death. Remember?" I handed her the sheet of paper. "They died coming to watch her play. I'm not saying I would quit playing, but I can see where she's coming from, I guess."

Emma stared at the news clipping. "Do you notice how she's all reserved?"

I knew exactly what she meant.

She finally looked up to meet my eyes. "Maybe if she played again, it would help. It could be like therapy or something."

"It would be cool to hear her play in person," I admitted, looking back at the screen.

"Oh, my god!" Emma exclaimed.

"What?" I asked in a quick breath.

"Look!" she said, pointing to my computer screen. "The date that video was uploaded is the same day her family died."

I looked back and forth between the article in Emma's hands and the video on my laptop. "Oh, my gosh. This is the concert performance her family was driving to see. She didn't even know. In this video, she probably thought her family was out in the audience, but they were already dead."

"That's so sad," Emma agreed quietly.

"Dinner," my mom called from down the hall, pulling Emma and me from the article and the beautiful tunes of one Sage Anderson.

***

After supper, Emma and I went through our normal routine, and I filled her in on what Teddy had told me. As much as I was motivated to learn more and start doing better with my abilities, it didn't feel like anything had changed.

You can't expect things to get better at the snap of a finger, I told myself after Emma left. *If only,* I thought, *then I'd be closer to figuring out this whole thing with Sage.*

It was getting late, but watching Sage play saxophone earlier had me itching to break out my own instrument. I rarely practiced—it's not like anyone else in our school band did—but our conductor made us bring our instruments home every night. I pulled my clarinet from my backpack and assembled it. I played through a few of the songs we were practicing for our spring concert, which helped me relax slightly before crawling into bed.

That night, I snuggled with my stuffed owl Luna for comfort and reached for my phone on my bedside table. I sent Robin a quick text—nothing special—and we stayed up texting for a while. I wanted to talk more about Sage, but I didn't know what to say. Nothing could be said that we hadn't already discussed. Eventually, Robin's texts stopped coming, and I assumed he'd fallen asleep.

Despite the late hour, I still couldn't bring myself to close my eyes and drift off to sleep. Too many worries raced through my mind. I thought about all the work I'd put into my abilities, but it didn't seem like I'd come very far. I replayed my mother's words in my head and pondered what they meant for my past and my future.

I didn't know how much time passed, but I still couldn't fall asleep. I thought long and hard about the other side and considered what was there. Did I get visions because of spirits, or was it something else? If it were spirits, who were they? Could it be possible that my dad was sending me messages?

I gripped onto my owl necklace and held onto that thought for some time as I wondered what it would be like if he was the one communicating with me. I pondered it so hard until I nearly believed it. A single tear ran down my cheek. I pulled Luna in close to my body in hopes of making my chest feel whole again. I couldn't help it. Whenever I thought about my father, a feeling of emptiness consumed me as if physically reminding me of the years he hadn't been here.

But what if he was here all along? I thought. *What if he's here now?*

"Daddy," I whispered into the darkness. I couldn't feel a spirit there. I had no way of knowing if my father could even hear me, but a little part of me wanted to believe it was possible, that if I spoke to him, he might actually help. After all, he had to be on the other side somewhere, right?

"Daddy, I feel so lost," I admitted to thin air in a quiet whisper. "I guess I'm ashamed of myself a little bit. Mom's right. I haven't put enough effort into my abilities, and it could cost a girl her life. If you're out there, Dad, will you help me save her? It's been days since my warning, and I haven't figured much out. I don't know how she's going to die. I don't know how to save her. Is her uncle coming for her? How can I fight against a full-grown man? You must know, right? Someone over there on the other side must know how to save her."

I took in a deep yawn as my eyes began to droop. "I don't have a whole lot of time left—just until the wedding—but I hope you'll be there for me when I need you, Dad."

After I let a few more thoughts go out to my father, I drifted off to sleep soundlessly.

12

I was restless at school on Thursday as I thought about what I might say to Sage if she came to Asher's again that night. I texted Robin to make sure he'd invite her again. He said he would, but all I could do was cross my fingers all day.

That night, Emma drove Derek and me to Asher's like before. I felt more comfortable this time as I settled into the now familiar basement.

"Is she coming?" I asked Robin quietly when I greeted him with a hug.

"She said she would." I could see the hint of sorrow in Robin's eyes. It was like he was already grieving for her. I knew he had faith in me, but at the same time, I understood how hard it was to talk about someone who you knew was likely to die soon.

Robin gave me a peck on the lips before he turned to tweak some of the equipment settings. I could see him stealing glances at me as he poked at things. I couldn't help but smile back at him.

"Troy." Emma positioned herself near Asher's younger brother on one of the couches. "Why aren't you in their band? Don't you play music?"

Faith, Troy's girlfriend, nearly choked on her laugh.

I took a seat on the opposite couch as I listened to the group talk. I was still waiting on Sage, but I didn't want to feel left out, either.

"Nah," Troy answered. "I love to hear them play, but I don't have that kind of talent. Imagine me playing guitar." He curled up his hand like he was holding an imaginary guitar. "My fingers just don't bend that way."

"And he can't keep a beat or sing in tune to save his life," Faith added.

"I'm more a visual artist, I guess," Troy said as he put an arm around Faith and pulled her close.

"What about you, Andrew?" Emma asked.

"Huh?" Faith's brother muttered, looking up from his phone. "Oh, yeah. I don't do this kind of stuff, but I play sax in the jazz band at school. It sounds nerdy, but it gets pretty intense there."

We all talked for a while to get to know each other. Eventually, we exchanged Facebook friend requests. Just as I accepted Andrew's friend request on my phone, I caught a glimpse of movement on the stairs.

"Sage!" I exclaimed a little too excitedly as I shot up from my spot on the couch. I quickly calmed my voice. "We saved a spot for you," I said dumbly, gesturing to the cushion next to me.

She smiled back sweetly. "So, uh, what are you guys doing?"

We all had our phones out and were huddled around the couches in a semi-circle, all except Robin and Asher, who were trying to fix a tuning problem on Asher's guitar.

Tyler twirled his drum sticks around his fingers. "Just falling victim to social media addiction," he joked. "Want to join?"

"It's okay," Sage declined, taking a seat next to me.

"What?" Tyler teased. "You don't use social media or something?"

Sage didn't say anything for a moment, and then she spoke softly. "No, I don't."

Even though Sage tried to stay casual, everyone but Emma, Derek, and me froze and stared at Sage like she'd just grown two heads.

"What?" Faith exclaimed. "How can you not use social media? My grandma is the only person I know who doesn't use social media, and that's because she's in a nursing home."

"Even our cat has a Facebook page," Andrew added.

I could see where this was going, and all I wanted to do was jump in and save Sage the trouble of explaining. I still didn't understand it completely, but I was sure it was something she didn't want to tell the whole room about. As if he could hear my prayer, Robin's eyes locked on mine from across the room. I tried my best to communicate a warning with my expression.

"Okay, guys," Robin announced.

I breathed a sigh of relief.

"We got the tuning problem fixed. Time to get started."

"What takes you guys so long to set up anyway?" Troy complained.

That started a whole string of snarky remarks from the band members until Robin got them to calm down again. Soon, they came together in harmony to play their songs to near perfection. Since I had downloaded their songs, I knew most of what they were playing. Some of them were new and weren't on iTunes yet. It was pretty clear since they weren't as good on those.

When they began playing a song I knew again, I couldn't help but sing along. I was pleased when I glanced over at Sage and she was moving her body to the music. That was the happiest I'd seen her since I'd met her. I almost turned away, but then I noticed her lips moving to the words.

"You know this song?" I asked above the music.

Sage pressed her lips together shyly. "They're on YouTube," she explained.

I smiled as I went back to singing the chorus.

Emma's voice rang loud above my own, even almost louder than Robin's. She had also downloaded their songs a while back and had memorized them all in under a week. I admired her ambition and courage to be heard in front of everyone.

"Hold on," Robin said into the microphone, stopping the music in its tracks.

Tyler was so surprised at the abrupt halt that he dropped his drum sticks.

Robin's eyes locked on mine almost aggressively. Had I done something wrong? What happened? "Crystal," Robin said, "you're in big trouble."

"What?" I asked in a way that came off sounding horrified.

"Why didn't you ever tell me Emma could sing?"

All the muscles in my body relaxed.

"We've been looking for female vocals, and here we knew a great singer all along. And it looks like she knows our songs."

"What?" Emma asked, enunciating the word. "Are you serious?" She made the question come off sounding like she wasn't up for it, but I knew Emma far too well. Inside, she was surely jumping at the chance to be part of a group like this.

"Yes, I'm serious." Robin held out his hand to her. "Come up to the microphone."

Emma glanced at Derek as if asking if she should.

Derek pushed at her. "Go on. It's only, like, your dream to sing in a rock band."

Emma smiled excitedly and hopped up from the couch. "What do I do?"

"Sing background vocals, of course," Robin instructed as he positioned her in front of a second microphone. He fiddled with it for a moment before it turned on. "You obviously know this song, right?"

Emma nodded. She tried to stay casual, but she was bouncing up and down slightly. A smile played at the corner of her lips.

"Think you can improvise a harmony?" Robin asked.

"I play harmony in band a lot, so I'm sure it can't be that hard."

Tyler interjected. "Those two look like they know what they're doing, too." He pointed a drum stick at Sage and me.

Sage and I exchanged a glance.

Robin smiled at us in a way that made my heart swoon. "You girls want to try it out, too? Just for fun?"

Sage and I looked at each other again. Her eyes lit up slightly.

"What the heck?" I shrugged, hopping up from the couch.

Sage planted a look of uncertainty on her face, but a part of her expression told me she was having fun. She finally rose from the couch, and we stood around Emma's microphone together.

"Okay," Robin said. "From the top."

Tyler beat on his drums, and suddenly the rest of

the basement came to life. I stood there stupidly for the first verse like I was unsure of myself. Honestly, though. Me? Singing? I wasn't much of a singer, but as Emma's voice grew louder, I couldn't help but let go of my insecurities and simply enjoy the beat.

Something about the moment gave me déjà vu. A memory played back through my mind, and I was pretty sure I had dreamt of this moment before. Was it possible that I was connected to Sage even before Melissa's warning?

I caught Sage's eyes opposite me, and she broke out into a full-on grin. I'd never seen Sage look so happy. The moment I realized this, nerves twisted in my stomach. Sage didn't have long. How many more happy moments would she have like this? Was I wasting her time with this whole band practice thing, or was it best that I let her be happy while she could?

"That was fun!" Emma exclaimed when the song ended. "Now go sit back down so I can try by myself," she teased, poking at me.

"Actually, I could really use something to drink," I said. It was true, but I was hoping for a moment alone with Sage again. "What about you, Sage?"

She smiled and tugged on her sleeves, balling them in her fists. "Yeah, sure. I'm pretty thirsty, too."

We escaped upstairs while the band began playing again. I pulled a cup from the dish rack and filled it with water, all the while wondering what I could say to her. I wanted to somehow ask if she was in danger—maybe from her uncle—but I didn't know how to bring the subject up lightly. The question of *how* she was going to die still nagged at me. I felt like if I knew that, I'd know how to save her, but then again, I knew *she* obviously didn't have that answer.

"Sage," I started, hoping this would work. "I've been wondering about something."

She took a seat at the kitchen table and popped open her soda can. "Yeah?"

I gently pulled out a chair next to her and sat down. "That thing you said earlier about not having social media profiles . . . Is there a reason for that? I mean . . ." I paused, looking down at my glass for a moment. "Are you in any danger or something?"

"What?" Sage laughed, but it sounded forced. "What would give you that idea?"

I shrugged. What was I supposed to tell her? That it was her dead sister who gave me that idea? I didn't have that sort of trust from her yet. As much support as I'd received from my family and friends, I knew telling a near stranger about my abilities probably wouldn't go over well.

"Nothing, I guess. I just wanted to make sure. I wouldn't want to miss a chance to help you if you were in trouble. Not that I think you are," I lied. My eyebrow twitched slightly. At least she wasn't aware that this was a clear indication of my dishonesty. "I just want to make sure because sometimes you do seem okay, but other times, it's like . . ." Now I was just babbling.

"Crystal," Sage said, stopping me. "I'm fine. Really. If I gave the impression that I was in any trouble, I'm sorry. I've just been really stressed lately."

I couldn't help but remember how it felt when I shook her hand that first day. She was scared of something. Was she still scared of it?

"Okay," I answered. I casually placed my fingertips on her exposed hand. "If you ever need anything, though, I am willing to listen."

I pulled my hand away, partially because I knew it was weird to touch her in the first place and partially because in the few seconds I was in contact with her, I didn't see a single thing. If there was something there, I should have seen it. At least that's what I told myself.

Sage sipped her Mountain Dew and then smiled at me. "Thank you, but I'm fine."

Even after Sage left, I still didn't believe her.

13

"I feel like I'm getting nowhere," I complained to Robin after Sage went home. Faith and Andrew were gone, too, and everyone else was up in the kitchen snacking on Asher's mom's homemade cookies. Robin and I sat together on one of the couches in the basement, his arm slung around me casually.

"Maybe you need to be more direct with her," he suggested.

"You mean, tell her that her dead sister warned me of her impending death? Tell her that her uncle might be coming for her? She'll call me crazy!"

"Has anyone called you crazy because of your abilities before, Crystal?" Robin brushed my blonde hair out of my face and looked me in the eyes as he asked this.

He was right. I'd told a good dozen people or more, and none of them had called me crazy. "In all fairness, I actually know everyone I told," I pointed out. "I don't really *know* Sage yet." Even as I said this, a small part of me believed Robin was right, so why was I so afraid to tell Sage when it could save her life?

"It may be worth a shot," Robin insisted. "I mean, I believed you, and we ended up saving Hope because of it."

I took a deep breath. "That's because I was able to prove it to you. What am I supposed to say to Sage? You can't just tell people they're going to die, Robin. Then it'd be like it was my fault."

"And if you didn't tell her and it happened anyway, would you regret it?"

I sighed in defeat. "You're right. I have to tell her. Beating around the bush isn't doing me any good."

"You know I'm here for you, right?" He kissed the top of the head. "No matter what happens. I care about Sage, too, so you don't have to feel like you're in this alone."

I nodded and pressed my head into his shoulder for comfort.

Robin gripped the bottom of my chin lightly and guided my face up to his. "I mean it," he said seriously before he pressed his lips to mine. I let myself fall deeper into the kiss until both our lips parted slightly.

Emma's footsteps on the stairs moments later made me pull away from Robin. I pressed my lips together in embarrassment, hoping that might stifle the blush rising to my cheeks.

"Crystal," Emma asked, bending from a higher step to get a good look at me, "are you almost ready to go?"

I nodded again and rose from my seat, still gripping onto Robin's hand. "So, I'll see you on Saturday at the park for Troy's birthday, then."

Robin stood up with me and stayed close. I could feel his breath on the top of my forehead as he looked down at me. It made the butterflies in my stomach spring to life.

"Will you invite Sage?" I asked. "Maybe I could talk to her more then. You know, about what we just talked about."

"Yeah," Robin said, closing the small gap between us. "I'll convince her to come. Have a safe ride home, okay?" He bent to my level again, pulling me into a passionate kiss.

"My eyes!" Emma exclaimed jokingly. When I turned to look at her to let her know I wasn't amused, one hand was covering her eyes. "My virgin eyes!"

"As far as I heard, there's nothing virgin about them," Robin joked back.

Emma froze for a second and looked at me with wide eyes as if to ask, *What did you say to him?* Not that Emma ever told me a secret on that topic.

Robin laughed. "I'm *kidding,* Emma. Chill."

She stood and pulled at the bottom of her shirt casually. "Well, yeah. I knew that."

I followed Emma upstairs and grabbed a cookie. "Oh, before I forget." I turned back to Robin, who had trailed behind me. "Do you guys want to do a double date sometime soon?" I remembered what my mom had said and figured I should follow her advice.

"Sure," Robin said with a cookie in his mouth. "Does Saturday night work for you?" He looked toward Derek and Emma, who both agreed.

"I'll be ready in a minute," Derek told us as he grabbed a few more cookies.

"Okay." Emma pulled at me. A look of *let's talk in private* crossed her eyes. On our way out the door, Emma spoke again. "So, still no 'I love you?'"

Thanks for reminding me, Emma, I thought. "It's not like you and Derek have said it, either."

"Actually," Emma announced proudly, "we have said it."

"What?" I practically choked on my surprise. "When?" I climbed into the back seat of Emma's car as she pulled open the driver's side door.

"Earlier this week."

"Why didn't you tell me?"

She shrugged. "I didn't really think about it until I realized you and Robin still haven't said it. It's not like you tell me everything."

"What are you talking about?" I asked, momentarily stung by the accusation. "I do tell you everything!"

"'About that thing we just talked about.' It's like

you didn't want me to hear whatever it was you and Robin were saying in private."

"No, it's not that," I insisted, feeling hurt that she'd think I would hide something from her. "He was just saying I should tell Sage about my abilities. Then there might actually be a chance at saving her."

Emma pressed her lips together in thought. "I don't know, Crystal. You don't really know her . . ."

"That's what I said, but I think he's right."

Derek's passenger side door opened with a click, and he climbed in. Emma and I both looked at him and went silent.

"Telling secrets, are we?" Derek joked.

I sighed because this whole decision about whether to tell Sage or not was stressing me out. "I was just getting Emma's opinion. What do you think, Derek? Should I tell Sage about my abilities or not?"

Derek shrugged. "I guess it's up to you, but it could just push her away."

"I know, but Robin thinks I should, and I trust him."

Emma started the car and pulled out of the driveway. "We're not going to tell you what to do, Crystal, but I *am* going to tell you I don't think it's a good idea."

I gazed out the window in thought. "But I'm not getting *anything* out of her otherwise. I have no idea what to ask or how to ask it. Everything I've found out is what Derek and Teddy told me. Fat lot of good my abilities are doing me."

Emma made a noise from the front seat. "Crystal, your abilities are really awesome. Don't say that."

I spent most of the rest of the car ride staring out the window wondering how Sage was going to die. Melissa had said that she didn't want Sage to "suffer the same fate." Did that just mean her death, or did it mean Sage was going to be in a car accident? And what was this whole thing with her uncle?

That thought reminded me to tell Derek about it. When he suggested we do a Google search on her uncle, I realized Teddy had never given me a name.

***

I took my time between Thursday and Saturday to think about what my friends had said, but even Friday afternoon at Hope's, I still felt completely lost. At least I'd gotten a name from Teddy, but I was unable to find anything on the right Alan Anderson. Why did Sage have to come from a family with such a common surname?

"Crystal." Hope snapped her fingers in front of my face.

"Huh?" My eyes refocused, pulling me from my thoughts. I gazed down at the Life board only to find that Hope already had another set of twins. I hadn't even gotten married yet.

"You seem out of it," she said.

I sighed. "That's because I am." I spun the Life wheel before looking back up to meet Hope's eyes. "It's just one of my friends," I started to explain, but I trailed off, wondering whether I should open up to Hope about this or not. I wasn't sure if she'd understand.

"Is she okay?" Hope asked, pulling a miniature husband out of the Life box for me.

"Not really," I admitted.

"Is it because you can see the future?"

I tensed. "What do you mean?"

"You found me because you can see the future, right?"

I relaxed and nodded. "I'm supposed to help this girl, but I don't know if I should tell her about my gift or not."

"If she's like me, she'll believe you."

"What do you mean?"

Hope straightened up and put a mature expression on her face. "The whole time I was missing, I dreamt about you. I knew who you were before you ever came to save me. Maybe your friend knows you're going to save her, too."

I thought about this for a moment, but it didn't make any sense that Sage knew. After all, when I helped my friend Kelli, she didn't know. "I don't think she's like you," I finally said.

"Well, I think you should tell her," Hope said, spinning for her turn.

Great. Now there was just one more opinion to add

to the confusion, especially since I was leaning toward not telling her.

On my walk home, I swung by Divination to get my mom's opinion since I knew she was working late and I might not get a chance to talk to her later. She always kept the shop open a little later on Friday nights, but there weren't any customers around when I entered.

As soon as I brought the subject up, my mom's entire demeanor changed. Her body tensed, and she wouldn't meet my gaze. She crouched down to a bottom shelf and reached into a box nearby to restock a few items.

"Mom," I prodded.

She sighed, stalling. "I've told you before what I think about you telling people." Her gaze finally reached mine.

I crossed my arms over my chest. *Not the answer I was looking for.*

She stood and pushed past me with her empty box. I followed her to the back of the shop.

"I'm not saying you can't tell her. It's not my job to tell you that, but you asked for my advice." She pushed open the door to the storage room. I followed, and the door clicked shut behind me.

"It's one thing to tell your best friends," she continued. "Even telling Robin made sense." She finally turned to me. "But if you start telling so many people, you're going to get too comfortable with it. Someday, you're going to tell the wrong person."

I wanted to roll my eyes at her, but with her next sentence, a sense of empathy washed over me.

"Believe me. I know."

I sighed and spoke softly. "So your vote is that I shouldn't tell her, then?"

"I can't tell you what to do, sweetie."

I gritted my teeth in exasperation. Aren't mothers supposed to have all the answers? She was really starting to sound like the mysterious gypsy she pretended to be every year for Halloween. "Well, if you were in the same situation, you wouldn't tell her, right?"

"I guess I'd have to be in that situation to tell. I don't know Sage well enough. The best thing I can tell you to do is to follow your instinct."

"Mom, I have no instinct. That's why I'm asking you. You're supposed to be my instinct."

She threw her head back and laughed. I couldn't help but let out a giggle with her.

She finally composed herself. "Once you're in the situation, you'll know what to do."

Why was she making this harder for me? "What would Sophie and Diane say?"

"Probably the same thing as me."

"Well, you guys are no help," I complained. My mom pulled me into a hug to calm my nerves.

"I can teach you about your abilities, Crystal. I can advise you against sharing your secret. But I can't tell you how you should feel. I won't tell you what to do. You know Sage better than I do. Do you think she'll believe you?"

Just then, the bells on the front door jingled, indicating a customer had just entered the shop. I let my mom tend to them, said goodbye, and headed home.

14

It was here: the moment of truth. I still didn't know what I was going to say to Sage, which only made me nervous on the car ride to the city.

"Crystal." Derek's voice brought me back to the present inside the car.

"What?" I asked, pulling my eyes from the scenery to meet his.

"What's wrong?"

"Nothing," I said as casually as I could. My eyebrow didn't even twitch this time. "What would make you think that?"

"Because you're chewing your nails like you're nervous."

I gazed down at my hands and realized he was right. The nail on my right ring finger was chewed raw.

"It's just . . ." I paused for a second. "Life," I finally said confidently. "It sucks being a teenage girl."

Emma and Derek both laughed from the front seat.

"I hear ya," Emma said, raising her hand in agreement.

I couldn't lie to them. "I'm still worried about Sage," I admitted. "I have a feeling the whole thing about her uncle being on the run is important, but given that the police don't know where he is, Teddy doesn't know anything else."

"Maybe Derek could work some of his detective magic," Emma suggested.

"Yeah," I agreed. "I tried finding him online, but Alan Anderson is a common name."

"I guess I could try," Derek offered.

"So, Emma," I started, trying to get back into casual conversation so they wouldn't worry about me. "Will you be up on stage today?"

She rolled her eyes. "I don't even know if I'm an official band member yet, and I haven't practiced with them enough."

"You'd love it, though," I told her.

"Maybe we could start our own band," Derek suggested with a laugh. The sad thing was that he sounded half-serious, and my only guess was that he didn't want to share Emma with a group of four other guys.

It was sunny with a light breeze when we reached the park. The last of the snow was gone, replaced with bits of spring greenery. I stepped out of the car and tugged slightly at the bottom of my hoodie as I looked around. There was a playground on one end of the park and a walking trail that went across a river and through the trees on the other side. I scanned the area for Robin but didn't see him anywhere.

"Where do you suppose they are?" Derek asked.

"Over there." Emma pointed. I followed her gaze and saw Asher's brother, Troy, under one of the pavilions. As we neared the shelter, I started to make out people I recognized, like Faith, Andrew, and Skip.

"Crystal," Robin greeted, embracing me and giving me a peck on the lips. Then he turned to Derek. "We're still getting some of the equipment out of the van. We could use another man if you're up for moving stuff."

Derek just shrugged and joined Robin to help. There weren't a lot of people there yet since we were technically early for Troy's birthday party, so Emma and I decided to take a stroll on part of the trail.

We talked as we walked, but the conversation remained casual. Eventually, we could hear Echo Score's beat coming from the pavilion the same time we met a fork in the path.

"It looks like if we go that way," Emma pointed to the left path, "it will take us back to the pavilion."

"Okay," I agreed, following her lead.

Just as we cleared the trees and spotted the pavilion again, I noticed a familiar figure making her way toward the music.

Sage.

"I'll catch up with you later, Emma."

She nodded and followed my gaze to Sage. "Are you going to tell her?"

I twisted my lips up in thought. "I don't know yet."

"Do you want someone there with you in case you do? I could, like, back you up."

I shook my head. "It's okay. Really. I don't even think I'll tell her, and no offense, but I think I have a better chance of learning more about her if I'm alone with her."

"It's okay. I understand." Emma gave me a cheerful wave as she broke away from me to go find Derek.

"Sage," I called as I caught up with her.

She smiled back at me. "I was looking for you. I don't really know anyone else here except Robin, but he's singing up there."

"It's kind of a relief hearing them out of the basement isn't it?" I joked. "It's not as deafening."

Sage chuckled. "So, uh, should we go meet some of Troy's friends, or will we just be those girls who sit in the corner?"

I let out a light laugh. "I'm okay with sitting in the corner, although that cake looks pretty tasty."

"Well, I won't say no to free food."

Sage and I grabbed some food and found our way next to Emma and Derek on one of the picnic tables. We all talked, laughed, and listened to the music for a while. When I stood to throw away my paper plate, I noticed that a small group of people had gathered on the side of the pavilion to listen.

"You know what we should do, Crystal?" Emma asked, grabbing my arm excitedly. She didn't wait for an answer. "We should dance to the music. It'd be good publicity for the band." She raised her eyebrows, pleading for me to join her.

"Seriously, Emma?"

"I know this line dance that would actually work really well with this song."

"Aren't line dances for country music?" I asked.

Emma shook her head. "Not all of them. Come on. It will be fun."

"Sounds fun," Faith cut in as she neared the trash can with her empty plate.

"What?" I asked.

"I'll help you, Emma," Faith said.

Emma jumped up and down excitedly. "Okay. I'll show you how to do it." She positioned herself near the front of the pavilion away from the picnic tables. "Hold on. Let me get the beat." She bobbed her head a couple of times before starting a grape vine.

After a few moments, Faith jumped in. "Oh, I know this one. You're right. It does work well with this song."

Dancing honestly *did* look like fun.

"I know this one, too," Sage said to me. "These guys taught it to me last summer at band camp."

I watched Emma and Faith hopelessly. "Well, I don't, so you'll have to teach me."

By now, another girl who I didn't recognize, but who seemed to know Faith, had joined in.

Sage slowly showed me how the dance went. After a few demonstrations, I told her to do it to the beat and I'd catch up. I didn't do so great as I watched Sage's feet move quickly, but I eventually started to get the hang of it.

When the song ended, we were all giggling while the onlookers actually gave us a round of applause.

"What now?" Sage asked when we sat back down at our picnic table. She tugged at her long sleeves and balled them into fists like she always did. I figured it was something she did in uncomfortable situations, and I was willing to bail her out of this one.

"Emma and I went for a walk earlier," I offered. "It was really pretty back in the trees. Want to go for a walk?"

"Sure," she agreed.

Once we neared the trees, Sage spoke again. "I actually walk through this park a lot, so I know how pretty it can get back here. But like I said, I haven't lived in the city long, so I haven't really seen it in full bloom yet."

"Why did you move to the city?" I asked. Even though I knew the answer, I figured a simple question like this would help her open up to me more.

She glanced at me for a moment and then locked her eyes back on the path. "I don't tell a lot of people this, but I feel like I can trust you. I can, can't I?"

"You can," I assured her.

"Okay, well . . ." She paused like she wasn't sure she wanted to tell me yet.

I looked at her for a moment and noticed her eyes turning red like she was holding back tears. Her voice cracked slightly when she spoke. "I moved here to live with my aunt and uncle."

"What about your other family?" I prodded. Was I doing this right, or was I overstepping?

Sage shook her head. "My family isn't around." She paused briefly. "Sometimes I feel like I'm all alone. My grandparents are all dead, and it just wouldn't work out to live with other relatives."

Her uncle, I thought. I only knew a small piece of that story, but I couldn't help but wonder what the rest of the pieces would tell me about her.

"You're not completely alone, though," I pointed out. "Your aunt and uncle must be pretty nice to take you in. And you have friends."

Sage gave an uncomfortable laugh. "They've been fine, but I don't think they understand what I'm going through." She didn't care to explain what she meant, but I already knew she was referring to her family's death.

She continued. "Brian—my uncle—just tells me to suck it up all the time. They don't have any kids yet—my mom was a lot older than her sister—so I don't think he really knows what it's like to be a dad yet. It's okay living with them, but I'm really glad Robin has been inviting me to these things. It's really sweet of you guys to include me."

A silence stretched between us because I didn't know what to say to that. You're welcome?

I was just about to answer when Sage tucked a strand of auburn hair behind her ear and spoke. "Can I ask you something?"

"Sure. Anything."

She tugged at her sleeves again. "Robin. Do you think he asks me to come to these things because he feels sorry for me?"

"No," I answered honestly.

"I guess I can't figure it out. He's known me all year and hardly said anything, and now he's constantly inviting me to these things. I mean, he practically begged me to take off work today to come. I just can't tell if he honestly thinks of me as a friend or not."

I bit my cheek nervously and thought about telling her the truth. Just then, we reached the fork in the path.

Sage pointed to the right this time. "If we go this way, there's a really pretty bridge. I could show you if you want."

"Okay. I haven't gone this way before."

My heart beat fast in my chest, telling me this was the moment. I knew I needed to tell her, but all the nerves twisting inside my belly made me want to chicken out.

"Actually . . ." I took a deep breath to help work up the courage to say something. "About Robin. He invited you because I asked him to."

Sage stared at me in surprise, but we didn't break our pace. "What? You didn't even know me. We met that one time."

"I know, but . . . I guess you just seemed like someone I could get along with."

I expected Sage to respond to that, but instead she said, "We're almost there."

The trees thinned slightly as we reached the bridge, which hovered over a small river with a steep bank. The greenery came to life around it with little pops of yellow and red along the water. I figured this river was a branch of the stream I spotted closer to the pavilion.

"You're right. This is really pretty."

"Oh, this isn't what I wanted to show you." She crossed the bridge and began making her way down the bank.

"Where are you going?" I looked toward the water nervously, afraid I'd slip and fall if I tried to make my way down there.

"It's okay. You won't fall," Sage assured me as she disappeared under the bridge.

I followed behind her. When I broke through the weeds and made it under the bridge, I found myself standing on a sort of sand bar that created a flat, dry platform.

Sage untied her shoes and dug her feet into the sand at the same time she plopped down onto it. "I come down here a lot to think. Something about it makes me feel safe, like no one could find me down here. As far as

I can tell, I'm the only one who ever comes here. There's some graffiti and stuff," she pointed up to the bridge, "but I've never run into anyone down here."

I took a seat beside her. "It is kind of peaceful, like a little hiding space. Well, a spacious hiding place."

"Yeah," Sage agreed. "But just so you know, if you tell anyone, I'm going to have to kill you." She faked a serious face, but she couldn't hide her smile.

"Cross my heart and hope to die." My heart sank at that thought. I should definitely not be making death jokes. The idea of it only brought a lump to my throat as I again tried to work up the courage to say something to her.

"You know what's funny?" Sage started before I could say anything. She leaned back on her hands and crossed her ankles to stretch out.

All I could do was pick at the bits of grass growing up through the sand. I didn't meet her eyes. "What's that?"

"I just told you one of my biggest secrets. Well, two actually. There's this place," she gestured around, "and then the fact that I live with my aunt and uncle."

I nodded for her to continue.

"Yet when I told you I was living with my aunt and uncle, you didn't ask why. It's all part of a bigger secret."

I froze for a moment. I knew how her parents died. Did that make me look suspicious? "That's private, isn't it?"

"I really would have thought the first time I told someone my own age that, they'd want to know why."

"Well . . ." I could hardly get the words out. My throat felt like it was closing up, and my brain was racing with questions about whether I should tell her the truth or not. My mother's voice echoed in my mind. Once I'm in the situation, I'll know what to do, she had said. I *wanted* to tell Sage. I swallowed and held my breath for a moment. It was now or never. "I actually do know," I finally admitted.

Sage's expression transformed into one of confusion. "How could you know?"

I continued picking apart the blade of grass in my hands, but it disappeared too soon. When that was gone, I pulled a small red blossom from the edge of the weeds and began plucking at its pedals. My voice wavered nervously as I spoke. "I wanted to add you on Facebook, but when I couldn't find you there, I turned to Google. I found the article about the accident." It wasn't the whole truth, but I didn't see a point in telling her my friends were involved, too.

"Oh," she said in understanding. "I didn't think they put my name in the article."

"They didn't, but some people from your hometown put it in the comment section."

"Oh. I guess I didn't really intend for anyone around here to find out."

"Why not?"

Sage shrugged. "I guess I don't want people feeling

sorry for me. They've done that for years, and I just thought I'd kind of get a new start with all of that when I moved here. After all, it's hours away from where I grew up, so it was kind of a relief that no one knew who I was or what happened to me. I like my aunt and uncle on one level because they kind of make me feel safe, and I need that while I'm finishing up high school. But I'm only with them until I graduate next month—I'm not 18 yet—and then I can go anywhere I want." She stared into the distance. "There are so many possibilities. That's why I work at Special Day Bridal. I'm saving up so I can get far away from here."

"What's wrong with Minnesota?" I asked.

Her eyes focused, and then she looked at me, but she didn't answer. Instead, she began picking apart her own blade of grass. After a long silence, she spoke again. "It was my fault."

"What?"

"The accident. My family wouldn't have died if it wasn't because of me."

"You can't blame yourself, Sage. The weather—"

"No. It was. You have to remember all that flooding we had last summer. Maybe you didn't have it around here. Anyway, I was at band camp, and my parents almost weren't going to come. But they couldn't reschedule the final performance, so I begged my family to come. I could have sworn I saw them in the audience, so I played my best for them, only afterward, I found out they never made it . . ."

Another silence settled under the bridge until I finally spoke. "If you think about it, they could have been there."

"What do you mean?"

I shrugged in an attempt to force nonchalance. "Like, in spirit, I mean."

Sage let out a breath of air that sounded a lot like a laugh to me. "You think that moments after their death, my family would have nothing better to do than to watch me play music? I'm sure if they were out there somewhere, they wouldn't be worrying about me."

Here's my chance, I thought. My pulse quickened as if in warning, but in the moment, I felt like something needed to be said. "But they are worried about you."

Sage went silent for a beat, and then she looked at me sideways. "You say that like you're sure of it."

My hands shook slightly, and the red blossom fell out of them. I closed my eyes for a few seconds to compose myself. "That's because I am." I forced down the lump rising in my throat. *This. Is. It.* "The first day I met you, I also met your sister."

There. I said it. Would she believe me? Would it save her? The following split second felt more like minutes. For a moment, I wasn't sure if admitting this was a victory or a mistake. I held my breath until Sage spoke.

"What are you talking about?"

"Melissa was there with me in the dressing room at Special Day Bridal," I confessed. "She told me that I needed to help you." I swallowed again, but the task was becoming more difficult as Sage stared at me in skepticism and my confidence in the situation plummeted. I locked my eyes on a rock near my toes.

"You mean to tell me . . ." Sage started slowly.

I wanted to take what I'd just said back because I could tell it was freaking Sage out, but the implication of my words was already out there.

"That I'm psychic? Yeah," I finished for her. "I know you probably don't believe me, but I can see ghosts and predict things about the future. I can even find things that people have lost or hidden, and sometimes when I touch people's skin, I can feel what they're feeling. You? You're scared of something." I finally lifted my eyes to meet her gaze, although I was terrified of her reaction.

The moments it took Sage to respond seemed to stretch into eternity. *Please believe me. Please believe me,* I chanted in my head. The seconds ticked by, taunting me and leaving me far too much time to wonder if this was the right choice or not. At first, I was sure it was bad, but then a glimmer of hope washed over me when she met my eyes.

"Oh, my god. You're crazy," she finally said.

My heart sank as I witnessed my worst fear come true.

"You actually believe that?" Sage asked, pushing herself to her feet. "I—I can't believe I brought you down here." She paused for a second, just long enough for tears to sting at my eyes. "I have to go."

"Sage, wait," I said, grabbing for her wrist to stop her. In that moment, fear consumed me. Fear. Sage was afraid of something, and this time, I knew what it was. *Me.* She was afraid of me.

"Please," Sage said, pulling away from me. The look in her eyes begged me to let her go, so I did.

15

I tried to hold back the tears, but the force at which they hit felt like a dam had broken inside of me. Sage's words cut into me like a knife, making me feel rejected.

You're crazy.

You're crazy.

You're crazy.

Can I really blame her for saying that, though? I thought the same thing when I learned about my abilities.

But the one thing that really ripped me apart was the thought that I'd failed. Sage wasn't going to talk to me again, so how was I supposed to save her?

I didn't know how long I stayed there, but I eventually calmed down enough, swallowed my pride, and crawled out from beneath the bridge. I wanted nothing more than to fall into Robin's arms and tell him what happened, about how I'd failed. He'd surely have something to say that would lift my spirits.

Luckily by the time I got back, the band was already packing up their equipment. The moment Robin saw my face, he ran toward me. "Where have you been, Crystal?"

Tears pricked at my eyes again.

"And where is Sage?"

"She left a while ago." I wrapped my arms around Robin's muscular frame for comfort. "I couldn't do it, Robin." My voice cracked. "I failed. I can't save her."

"Crystal," he said, pushing my hair out of my eyes to look into them. "What are you talking about? What happened?"

I took a deep breath and finally composed myself. My voice came out surprisingly even given the circumstances. "I told her like you said I should. I told her I was psychic. Robin, she called me crazy and said she didn't believe me."

He pulled me into a deeper hug. "I'm sorry I encouraged you to tell her. So, she knows she's going to die, then? Or at least that you think she is?"

I ran the conversation back through my head and realized I'd never mentioned that. "Actually, no. I told her about her sister and that I saw her." I paused for a moment. "I get where she's coming from, but I just—I wish it would have gone better."

Even as I said it, I wasn't sure how much I did

understand where Sage was coming from. After all, I hadn't been through what she had. Sure, I'd lost my dad, but there was always someone there to support me 100 percent. The more I thought about it, the more I realized that the overwhelming amount of support I had in my life had clouded my judgement. Everyone I had told about my abilities had accepted them, but with the pain of rejection coursing through my veins now, I finally understood—if only slightly—why my mother insisted I be careful about who I tell.

"Maybe I took it too far," I admitted to Robin.

He didn't say anything. He just took my hand and led me back to the vehicles next to the pavilion. At the same time, Emma was already making her way toward us.

"Crystal, are you okay?" she asked once we met up. She rested a hand on my shoulder for comfort. "It didn't go well, huh?"

All I could do was shake my head. We reached the vehicles, and I leaned against the band's van for support.

"Sage didn't believe her," Robin explained in a low voice.

Emma opened her mouth like she was going to speak, but then she closed it. I figured she was ready to gloat about being right until she noticed how much it was really bothering me.

Derek showed up next to Emma a second later and placed his arm around her shoulder. "What's wrong?"

he whispered to Robin, who promptly explained the situation.

I kept my gaze locked on a pebble in the parking lot. Sage's words played over and over in my head, and for several long minutes, it was the only thing I could focus on. Even my vision blurred as symphonies of *You're crazy* played through my mind. Next to me, I was sure my friends were discussing Sage, but I didn't process anything they said.

"Crystal." The sound of my name pulled me back into focus. I looked up to meet Emma's gaze. "So, how about that date?"

I forced a half smile. Would that solve anything? Was it fair to enjoy myself when I still didn't know how Sage was going to die? It felt like in the last hour I'd just taken ten steps backward. I didn't respond, but my thoughts were clearly written all over my face like normal.

"You realize you don't need her to believe you in order to save her, right?" Derek pointed out.

"What do you mean?" I asked.

Robin was the one to explain. "Just keep using your abilities, and then be there when it's going to happen."

I blinked a few times, absorbing this idea. "Robin, she's supposed to die on my mom's wedding day." I didn't know why I felt the need to point this out. On one level, I felt like I couldn't abandon my mom. On another, I knew I wouldn't abandon Sage when her life depended on me.

"You're right," I said after a long silence. "I don't need her to believe me. I just have to figure out what's going to happen, and then I'll know how to stop it. At least I know when. I still need to know where and how."

Robin smiled at me encouragingly. "That's what I like to hear," he said, leaning in and kissing the top of my head. "Remember we'll always be here to help. We're all concerned about Sage, but unlike you, *we* believe in your abilities."

I smiled back at him. He was right. Maybe I didn't need Sage to believe in me, but as long as my friends believed in me and I was just as confident, anything was possible.

"Like Robin said, we're all just as worried about Sage as you are." Somehow I doubted that, but Emma continued. "We're going to help you save her, but I think you need to take your mind off Sage for a few hours." Emma sounded strangely like my mom.

Taking my mind off Sage wasn't easy, especially because it felt like I'd just pulled a knife out of my heart, but when I snuggled into Robin's arms in the back seat of Emma's car, I found the task much easier. I was grateful for all the psychic practice I'd done in the last few months in learning how to control my thoughts and body. It allowed me to put Sage out of my head the way my mom told me I needed to do.

"So, do we know what we're doing?" Emma asked as she pulled out of the parking lot.

"Well, we all just ate," Derek pointed out, "so I'm

not hungry or anything."

"Crystal," Robin asked, "what do you want to do?"

"Hmm . . ." I thought. "Something fun?"

"Well, duh," Emma said from the front seat.

"A movie?" Derek suggested.

Robin crinkled his nose. "I don't know of anything good out right now. We could go bowling or something like that."

Emma weaved through the city streets. "Well, I'm going to just keep driving around until someone tells me what to do."

Everyone fell silent for a minute as we all pondered ideas. "What about something like laser tag? Or maybe paintball?" I suggested.

Emma drew in an excited breath. "That sounds like a lot of fun! Is there a place like that around here?"

"Yeah." Robin resituated himself closer to Emma to give her directions.

We drove past the city limits and out to a secluded paintball arena. There was a forest on one side and the familiar flat cornfield of southern Minnesota on the other. The arena itself was spread across an enormous field and dotted with inflatable bunkers. Before I knew it, I was suited up, an employee was handing me equipment, and we were being ushered into the arena. We were up against what must have been a 12-year-old's birthday party.

"This is a game of elimination," the employee explained to us. "Each team will start at their respective bases. From there, you're free to roam the arena. Once you've been hit, you'll go to the elimination zone," the guy gestured to a section off the field, "and wait for the next round to start. Everybody good?"

When no one had anything to say, we entered the field and took our bases. When the employee announced it, the game was on. I stood there like a fool, trying to take in my surroundings. Emma and Derek were already gone, and our enemies had scattered.

"Crystal," Robin said in a low voice, "what are you waiting for?"

I scanned the area again and immediately spotted one of the boys aiming his gun straight for my chest a few bunkers away.

"Run," Robin shouted, pulling me after him. He never was one for physical activity because of his leg, but he managed to react quickly enough to dodge the kid's paintballs.

The paintball flew past me as I dove for cover behind a second bunker. I couldn't help but laugh in relief.

"What's so funny?" Robin asked.

I shrugged. "I don't know what I'm doing."

"It's all about strategy. Follow me."

Robin stayed low as he peeked around the corner. I could hear the boys running around the arena and yelling at each other. One was barking orders while the others laughed in exhilaration.

"This should be easy." I grinned mischievously. It

was only a minute into the fight, and I was already starting to relax. It was easier to put Sage out of my mind when I could channel my feelings in a game of war.

"I hear one coming," Robin whispered. "Are you ready?"

I nodded.

On his signal, Robin and I jumped from behind our wall of safety.

Pop, pop, pop.

Each of Robin's paintballs hit the boy square in the chest. One of mine managed to catch him in the leg.

The boy fell to his knees and dropped his gun. "I've been shot!" he exclaimed dramatically as he clutched his chest and fell to the ground. In a struggling whisper, he managed to say, "Tell my mother I love her."

Robin and I exchanged a glance. Was the kid just taking this thing too seriously, or did we actually hurt him?

"Dude," Robin said, standing above him. "Are you okay?"

The kid opened one eye. In one swift motion, he grabbed his gun, sprung up from the ground, and shot Robin twice in the shoulder.

"I'm fine, sucker," the kid shouted before running away.

I couldn't help but let out a laugh.

Robin rolled his eyes at me. "Okay, I'm not falling for that one again." Then he turned to yell at the kid.

"That doesn't count. You were already eliminated!"

"Awe, but it was funny," I laughed.

"Keep laughing and you're getting one of these," he wiggled his gun, "straight to the chest."

I shut my mouth immediately but couldn't hide my smile.

"Come on. Let's go kick some butt." Robin took my arm again and led me behind another inflatable bunker. He put his finger to his face to tell me to be quiet.

At the same moment, I heard footsteps behind me. I whirled around and brought my gun to my shoulder but relaxed when I realized it was just Derek. He was already covered in blotches of paint.

"You look dead," I joked.

"Ha ha," Derek said sarcastically as he continued on his way to the elimination zone. "Let me know how it feels once you've been eliminated."

Robin peeked around the side of the bunker to get a good look while I crouched down low, waiting for him to tell me what to do. After what seemed like several minutes, he cocked his finger at me, and I followed behind him. We quickly shuffled across the field and ducked behind another bunker.

I spotted movement from one of the other team members and fixed my eye on the bunker I thought I saw him dive behind. The next thing I knew, the kid emerged from his hiding spot and began racing straight toward me. I fired a few shots, but they all exploded helplessly in the grass around the kid's feet.

"Run." I pushed at Robin, and we both took off.

He positioned himself behind a smaller bunker and shot at the boy to cover me while I headed for my own hiding spot. I'd always been a fit person, but as I closed the distance to my target bunker, my breathing quickened and became shallow, like my lungs were closing up.

Suddenly, the scene shifted around me. The green of the grass faded into the pale gray of concrete, and the bunkers surrounding me transformed into tall buildings. People milled around me, but I pushed through the busy crowd, never slowing. My mind completely detached from the paintball arena. All I knew on this busy street—one I didn't even recognize—was that if I didn't keep running, something bad was going to happen to me. I glanced behind me to make sure I wasn't being followed, but I didn't see anyone. Still, I sprinted forward to save myself, dodging people the entire way.

I rounded a corner and finally emerged from the crowd. With a free stretch down the secluded street, I sprinted as fast as I could. It felt like I'd never run so fast in my life the way my legs protested and burned. I took a huge gulp of air, but it felt like a weight was crushing down on my lungs. I couldn't stop now. I spotted an area of trees and ran for cover.

A moment later, I found myself back in my paintball gear complete with a gun in my hand, but the arena was gone. I removed my helmet and looked around frantically. What had just happened? Trees surrounded me in a thick forest, but through them, I caught a glimpse of the blue and red bunkers.

Leaves crunched next to me, and I immediately brought my gun up to my shoulder. I recognized the figure making its way toward me.

"Robin?" I asked, lowering my weapon. "What happened?"

"I don't know," he said, slowing his pace until he was standing right next to me. "You just took off, but you were running so fast, I couldn't catch up. Are you okay?"

The look on my face must have answered his question because in the next moment, he dropped his gun and pulled me into his arms.

"Crystal, what's wrong?"

I blinked a few times to hold back the tears. "I have no idea. I—I think I just had a vision. I was being chased."

"Well, you were being chased," Robin told me, although there was a hint of sympathy to his voice. "That kid was chasing you down, and then you left the boundaries of the arena, so I came after you."

I shook my head. "I don't mean it like that, Robin. I wasn't . . . here. I was in the city somewhere, but I didn't recognize it."

"Do you think it has to do with Sage?"

That hadn't even occurred to me. "What? I—I don't know. Why do you think that?"

"Because your visions always mean something. If not about Sage, then what?"

I remained silent in his arms for what seemed like several minutes while digesting this and playing the vision back through my head. Maybe if I could talk with Sage again, I could figure out what it meant, but would she talk to me?

"Maybe it's, like, a metaphor," I suggested. "Like, Sage is trying to run away from something, but I mean, I already knew that. She's clearly trying to escape the memory of her family's death, and she says she wants to get out of the city once she graduates. But the thing is that she probably won't talk to me again."

"Maybe I could try talking to her."

I hugged Robin tighter. "Would you? I mean, I just don't want her to see me as a freak. She doesn't have to believe me, but I still feel like I need to be around her to protect her."

Robin pushed my hair out of my face. "I'll try to get her to come around." Then he took my hand. "Come on. Let's get back to the arena, and we can turn our stuff in."

When we made it back, Emma and Derek were both splattered with paint. Since the kid shot Robin in the shoulder, I was the only one paint-free.

"Crystal, what's wrong?" Emma asked immediately.

"I'll tell you about it in the car. Can we just go?"

As we rode home, I realized that my mom was right. Taking the time to relax *did* help me with my abilities, but I still didn't know what the vision meant. That sent a nervous shutter throughout my body.

16

On Sunday, I spent my time helping my mom with last-minute wedding plans in hopes of taking my mind off Sage again so I'd see something worthwhile, but it didn't get me anywhere. Mom, Sophie, Diane, and I sat around the kitchen table putting together the centerpieces for the wedding.

"Sophie? Diane?" They both looked up at me expectantly. "Have either of you two seen anything about Sage?" I kept my gaze on the ribbon I was measuring out.

Out of the corner of my eye, I watched Sophie set down her centerpiece. "I'm sorry, Crystal, but I haven't seen anything except what I felt that first day."

"I've been trying, too," Diane said, "but there's nothing."

"And Teddy doesn't have any more insight?" I asked, although I knew he would have told me if he did.

My mom shook her head.

"Maybe we could postpone the wedding," I joked with a nervous laugh. Would that even work? Melissa said Sage would die when I wore the dress. If we postponed it, all that would do was postpone Sage's death, and by that point, I may still not have any more answers. My heart sank at the joke. "I didn't mean that. I'm sorry. But maybe we could hire her a body guard." I suggested half-seriously. "Or talk to the police."

My mom shook her head again. "What would we say? 'Officer, my daughter and I are psychic, and we need you to protect a girl we know because her dead sister told us to.'"

I knew how silly it sounded. If we lived in a world of logic, there'd be no real reason to worry about her. No one would believe us if we told them she was in danger.

"Sweetie." Sophie inched closer to me, and I raised my head to meet her gaze. "Being psychic is a lot harder than how Hollywood portrays it. With things like this, it's usually a one-girl mission, which is a shame, and rarely will you be able to control anything you see. But you should know that if you have any questions, we are *always* here to answer them."

"Okay." I set my project down. "I don't understand why I can control some things and not others. Like, if I want to find lost keys, I can do it like *that*." I snapped my fingers. "If I want to feel someone's emotions, I can usually do it just by touching them. I can even tell when it's going to rain. But things like seeing the past and the future, or even ghosts, is totally out of my control. Is there any way *to* control it?"

"Crystal," my mom said, "remember that you've only been at this for a few months. I mean, we're all surprised at how far you've come in such a short amount of time." They all exchanged a glance in agreement. "But it will take you years to be remotely close to controlling things like that. Finding things doesn't take a lot of energy, but looking into the past and the future is harder."

"Just keep practicing," Diane encouraged, "and things will get easier."

I nodded. "Yeah, I know you guys are right, but with everything the universe has thrown at me in the last few months, with Kelli, Hope, and Sage, it would just make more sense if it'd show me more at one time."

"Maybe it's trying," my mom pointed out. "You just have to make sure you're listening." There it was again. That accusation, like I didn't *care* enough about my abilities. Her voice was soft and kind, but her words cut into me like a razor blade.

I didn't say another thing. We finished the centerpieces, and then I shut myself in my room. I couldn't believe my mom didn't think I cared about my abilities. Was she *serious*? I gritted my teeth in frustration.

Setting out to prove her wrong, I spread my yoga

mat out at the foot of my bed. Hours passed as I let go of expectation and connected with the other side. I knew I wanted to see something, but I gave myself permission to not care if a vision came or not. Even after darkness enveloped my room and I finally opened my eyes, I still hadn't seen anything, but the fact that I was doing something to improve my abilities by getting in tune with them left me with a sense of comfort as I crawled into bed.

***

On Monday, Derek, Emma, and I chatted quietly in geometry as Mr. Bailey left us to our own devices.

"So I did some research," Derek said.

"About your parents?" Emma asked excitedly. "Do you know how they died yet?"

Derek shook his head and kept his voice low. "No, I'm talking about Sage."

I leaned in closer to the center of our little triangle in intrigue.

"You guys were talking about her uncle before, Alan Anderson. I spent pretty much all day yesterday looking for him online. I tried out different spellings of the name, narrowed the geographical area, and all that."

"And?" I prodded.

"I honestly didn't come up with much. I found some public records, but that's basically things we already know, like that he's a fugitive. Other than that,

I found that he used to work construction, and the best I can tell, he's never been married." Derek pulled a sheet of paper from between the pages of his notebook. "This was the only picture I could find of him online, but it has to be pretty old."

Alan didn't look all that scary, with soft brown eyes and a sweet demeanor. Except I knew what he had done, and that frightened me. I handed the photo back to Derek. "Okay, so we don't know anything more about him really, but do you guys think he's important in some way? I mean, do you think I should waste any time caring about him? He's probably long gone."

Emma shook her head lightly like she wasn't sure. "I don't know . . . I think it has to mean something. I mean, at least it explains why Sage is so reserved and kind of shy."

Derek twisted his mouth in thought but didn't say anything.

I recalled the way my mom said that sometimes the universe is trying to tell me something but I just don't listen. What if this was one of those times? "Actually, Derek. Can I keep that photo?"

"Sure," he said, handing it over.

I folded it up and slipped it into my backpack after class.

***

That afternoon, I picked Hope up from school and

walked her home like normal. Today, she wanted to play Go Fish.

"Crystal," she said in a scolding tone after she dealt. "You're distracted. Is it your friend again?"

I finally met her gaze and realized I hadn't even picked up my cards yet. I didn't even know what I was thinking about, but she was right. I was distracted. "It's—yeah. It is my friend. It's—" I couldn't decide if I should tell Hope or not. I mean, she knew about me and everything, but she was still so young. "I'm kind of on a time limit to figure something out, and I'm running out of time. Not to mention that my friend won't talk to me anymore."

"You could always, like, peer into your crystal ball to see what to do," Hope suggested jokingly. That immediately brought up an idea I couldn't believe I hadn't thought of before.

As soon as I entered my house, I rushed to my room. I had intended to use my crystal ball a week ago, but it had gotten buried under my pile of clothes in my messy room. I threw shirts out of the way until my hands clamped around a rock-hard object. My heart beat madly in excitement as I set the ball back on its stand. I wanted to get started right away, but I knew nothing would come of it. I needed to calm down first. I took a deep breath but was still twitching in anticipation. I needed a quick break before I tackled this. Emma would be here soon, and we'd "get in the zone," so I figured I could try the crystal ball after Emma left. I needed the privacy.

I made my way to the kitchen to find that Teddy was almost done preparing food. I took a seat on one of the stools along the counter. My mom wasn't anywhere in sight, so I figured she was still at the shop. Since she owned it, it was always somewhat unpredictable when she'd be home.

"Teddy?"

He looked at me expectantly. "Yeah? Is something wrong, Crystal?"

What would give him that idea? As soon as I asked myself the question, I realized I was biting the corner of my lip and clutching the owl pendant around my neck. I relaxed.

"I guess I was just kind of wondering if you knew anything else. You know, about Sage."

Teddy stirred the soup he was making. "I wish I could say I did, but you already know everything I know. As far as Sage's uncle, the police have been looking for him for nearly five years, and nothing's come of it. If it's not in the records, I don't know anything."

"What about . . ." I trailed off.

"What about what?" he asked curiously.

"I mean, you don't have a feeling about any of this or anything?"

"You mean, like, a supernatural feeling?"

I nodded.

He gave a slight laugh. "Crystal, I don't know how

much my 'feelings' would help in a situation like this. I've always been intuitive, but nothing like you and your mother."

I nodded in understanding. "You don't think Sage's uncle has anything to do with my warning, do you?" I didn't even know if *I* thought that, but it was information connected to Sage nonetheless.

"Do you want my professional opinion?" Teddy didn't wait for an answer. "I really don't think Sage is in any danger from him right now. A guy like that wouldn't come out of hiding after so many years for risk of being caught, unless he felt guilty about what he'd done. But in that case, he wouldn't hurt Sage. The truth is, he's probably changed his name and face and is long gone."

I thought about this for a moment and knew Teddy was probably right. "I guess that makes a lot of sense. If you come up with anything else, you'll tell me right away, right?"

"You bet," he said before he turned back to the soup.

A few minutes later, Emma arrived. I ate my soup and then joined her in my bedroom. My thoughts were on my crystal ball, but I knew I had to get through the relaxation part of everything before that would even work.

Today, it was the same thing as normal, except Emma stayed a while longer so we could finish up our geometry homework together. When she left, I felt ready to connect with my crystal ball.

I situated myself at my desk and took several long, deep breaths then hovered my hands over my crystal ball.

I couldn't tell how much time passed as I sat there focusing on my breathing.

In.

Out.

No expectations.

In.

Out.

No expectations.

I repeated this mantra in my head. My shoulders relaxed, and my eyelids fell into a comfortable, closed position.

In.

Out.

No expectations.

Soon, the mantra lost all meaning, and my mind cleared completely. A feeling of tranquility overcame me so much that I felt I wasn't even conscious, like I was peacefully dreaming. At some point, though, a voice in the back of my head told me to open my eyes. When I did, my crystal ball was glowing. A wave of beautiful colors emanated from the ball, dancing in a serene motion that pulled me in. I leaned toward it, magnetized.

My nose hovered inches above the ball as an image began to take shape. At first, it was all just a cloudy mess, but then the cloud transformed into flames. Each flame rippled in the image, like fingers trying to claw their way out of the glass. As soon as I saw them, the flames took the shape of solid fingers. The bright orange glow darkened to a deep red. Crimson liquid pooled in the hand and ran off it in drips.

No, I thought, horrified. The moment the terror consumed me and an intense fear rippled throughout my body, the swirling colors in the crystal ball disappeared. It returned to normal, like it was just an ordinary decoration.

I quickly pushed myself away from my desk to put distance between myself and the ball, nearly toppling over in the process. I buried my face in my hands, and my body heaved with dry sobs.

No, no, no, I thought.

The reality of the situation hit me hard and stayed there, like a weight was pulling me down. My breath ceased to the point where I had to remind myself I needed air. My breathing wavered as I swallowed the lump in my throat and faced the dire truth of the situation.

Unless I did something to save her, Sage was going to die a gruesome death.

17

Each sunrise over the next few days felt like a countdown in a ticking time bomb. It was less than three weeks until the wedding, and a sickening feeling consumed me as each preparation we made for it felt synonymous to a step closer to Sage's death. The question of *how* she was going to die still aggravated me.

Most of my time was spent trying to come up with a way I could save Sage when she wouldn't hear what I had to say. The least I could do was try to get her to come around, so that Tuesday morning, I tried calling her in hopes of getting her to come back to the band practice that night. She didn't answer, so I called Robin.

"Hello?"

"Hey, Robin. I was just curious how it went with Sage yesterday at school. Did you talk to her?"

"I tried, but she didn't say much," he admitted.

I sighed, and then I jumped into the explanation about what I saw in my crystal ball.

"That's really freaky. I will definitely try to talk her into coming tonight, but I mean, I can't make any promises."

"I know."

"But you know what?" Robin said. "Even if she doesn't want to talk to you, you're still going to save her. You know that, right?"

I didn't answer because in all honesty, I *didn't* know that. Was it going to be a car crash? Was her uncle coming for her? Was it something else entirely?

I still didn't know her all that well. If I could warn her . . . But how could I warn her when I didn't know what to warn her about? She wouldn't listen to me anyhow, would she?

"I hope you're right," I finally said. "I— " I stopped, realizing for a moment that I almost told him I loved him. It was the truth, wasn't it? But I couldn't bring myself to say it first. "I'll see you tonight."

***

"She'll be okay," Robin promised after his band practice. "She has you on her side."

Sage hadn't shown up for practice, and I was positive it was because she was scared of me.

"But how exactly do I help her? What, am I

supposed to stalk her on my mom's wedding day?"

Robin's eyes shifted in thought.

"I can't miss my mom's wedding. Am I supposed to tell her to cancel? It's not like I can get Sage to come to the wedding, not when she won't even come to your band practice anymore."

Robin rubbed my arms for comfort. "You don't know she didn't come because of you."

"Did she tell you why she wouldn't come?"

"She just said she was busy."

"That's textbook translation for, 'Your girlfriend is a freak, and I don't want to be around her.'"

"Hey," Robin said softly, kissing me lightly on the lips. "She might still come around."

I wanted to believe Robin's words, but when Thursday came and Sage still wasn't there, I knew he was completely wrong about that. Even so, I found myself half-believing his idea that I could still save Sage despite her need to avoid me. I wasn't entirely convinced, but at least there was a glimmer of hope.

"What do you guys think I should do?" I asked Emma and Derek when we piled into the car Thursday night. My social studies homework was spread across my lap in the back seat, but I couldn't pay attention to it while this question rattled around in my brain.

"About what?" Derek asked, twisting in his seat to look at me.

"Sage clearly doesn't want to talk to me, but I still have to save her. I don't know how she's going to die—

even with that freaky thing I saw in my crystal ball. So, how do I make sure she's safe on my mom's wedding day?"

"You could tell her not to leave the house," Derek suggested.

I slammed my textbook closed in annoyance. "I just said she won't talk to me, and even if she would, she wouldn't believe something like that."

Derek held his hands up in defense. "Hey, you asked for suggestions . . ."

I sighed deeply. "Yeah, I know. I'm sorry. That wasn't a personal attack, Derek. It just seems like nothing is going to work."

"I'd say you should invite her to the wedding," Emma said, "so she would be safe, but like you said, she may not agree to it."

A brief silence filled the car as we all worked to come up with a solution, but I couldn't stand the silence.

"It's not just that that's annoying me. I mean, all of this . . . I still don't know how she's going to die. I mean, if I did, I could prevent her from, say, crossing the street, or getting into a car, or doing whatever freaky thing is supposedly going to kill her. But it's not even just that, either." I reached for my backpack and unzipped the front pocket. "I still can't figure out what Sage's uncle has to do with all of this."

I unfolded the paper and studied the man's face, using the headlights of the car behind us to illuminate his features. "And there's so much left unanswered with him. Like, I get why he's on the run, but what prompted it? And how far did he run? And is Sage in danger from *him*? And if she is, what do I do about it?"

Neither Emma nor Derek said anything. They both just shrugged their shoulders like they didn't know what to say.

When the car went silent again, I rested my head against the window and stared at the photograph of Alan. His involvement was shrouded in so much mystery. The longer I looked at him, the drowsier I became, and at some point on our way back home, the exhaustion overtook me.

***

The day I told my mother was the most terrifying day of my life. I didn't want to tell her because I knew he would kill me if I did.

"You won't tell anyone, will you, Sage?" he had said the first time.

All I could do was look up at him in terror and shake my head in agreement.

"Good. Because you know what will happen if you do?"

The fright I felt for my uncle caused my throat to close up. I could hardly breathe, let alone speak. I shook my head.

"I'll kill you." He said it like it was a joke, but I was in no state of mind to take the words lightheartedly. "You understand, then, right?"

I nodded as bile rose to my throat. I forced it down, along with my disgust for my uncle, because that was the only way

I figured I'd survive.

But even though I'd never said anything, my mom somehow knew. I lied to her at first, but at 12, I could read her expression well enough that I knew she'd caught on and wouldn't accept my refusal.

My mother sat me down in her bedroom and spoke to me lightly. "Sage, I need you to tell me the truth. It's really, really important. Is Uncle Alan hurting you?"

Tears rose to my eyes. "No," I said without meeting her gaze.

"Are you sure?" My mother's eyes bore into mine in a way I'd never seen before.

I nodded.

"You'd tell me if he was, wouldn't you?" she asked.

I thought about this for a moment. How long could I keep lying to her? It was only a matter of time before someone witnessed something. I blinked a few times, considering telling her the truth. If I did, my uncle had promised he'd kill me, but was that any worse than what he was already doing to me? Was it worth keeping up this lie just to save my own life? Wouldn't it hurt less once all this was over? In that moment, I decided that I'd rather die than continue lying about it.

Slowly, like I was still thinking about the decision to give up the lie, I shook my head at my mother. She pressed her lips into a thin line, and her eyes grew red like she was going to cry.

That night, my mother told Melissa and me she was taking us to the movies. I wasn't stupid. I knew it was just a way to get us out of the house. But we didn't make it out the door before my uncle came home and I heard my father's confrontation with him.

"What the hell were you thinking, Alan?" I heard him say. "They're my daughters. *You're a sick bastard. And after everything we've done for you? We put a roof over your head! You're no longer welcome in this house. Not now. Not ever!"*

I heard the thud as my father's fist connected with my uncle's jaw. I exchanged a horrified glance with Melissa the same time my mother pulled us both into a hug. Tears ran down all of our cheeks.

Six more thuds reverberated through the walls before I heard the roar of my uncle's pick-up truck spring to life.

My uncle never came back to our house, but every time I closed my eyes, he was there in my nightmares.

***

My eyes shot open, and I gasped for air.

"Crystal?" I heard Derek's voice say.

I swung my head around, trying to figure out where I was. It was dark, and I was moving. After a moment, I realized I was still in the car. I clutched my hand over my chest as my heartrate slowed.

"What was that? Are you okay?" Derek asked.

"I—" I thought about it for a second.

On one level, I was freaking out at the terror I felt in Sage's memories. On another level, I'd *seen* something, and although it wasn't directly connected to Sage's death, it left me feeling one step closer to helping her.

"I'm fine," I answered truthfully.

18

The weekend passed like any other—uneventful—although a sense of worry taunted me as Saturday marked just two weeks until Sage's death. As guilty as it made me feel, I didn't know what else to do but wait and hope for the best.

Monday came with good news.

Talked to Sage, Robin's text said during lunch. *Says she's not mad at you.*

I had to wonder exactly what that meant. Did it just mean she was trying to get rid of Robin and stop his inquisition, or did it mean she was interested in talking to me again? All I could do was cross my fingers and hope she would show up to Robin's band practice on Tuesday. I wasn't keeping my hopes up too high. That's why I was shocked when my phone rang on Tuesday on our way to the band practice and Sage's name came up on the caller ID.

"Hello," I greeted, almost too quickly.

"Crystal?" Sage's voice came across the line.

"Yeah."

"Hi." She paused for a moment like she didn't know what to say. I heard her take a deep breath. "Let me start by saying I'm really sorry."

"About what?" I asked, feigning ignorance. It came across sounding fake, even to me.

"You know exactly what I mean. I shouldn't have called you crazy. Anyway, I just wanted to let you know I was sorry."

"So, you're coming to the band practice?" I asked, almost with too much enthusiasm.

"Actually," Sage said, her voice coming off a little shy like usual. "I was hoping you'd accept my apology over dinner or something, if you haven't eaten yet. We could meet at the food court in the mall. I'm more in the mood for a girls' night instead of hanging out with all of Robin's friends. Not that there's anything wrong with them. But only if you don't mind."

"No!" I nearly shouted. "I don't mind. I'm almost to the city. I can be there in about 15 minutes. Does that work for you?"

"Yeah! I'll see you soon."

I hung up. "Emma, is it okay if you drop me off at the mall? Sage wants to meet up with me there. You guys don't think it will be weird being at Asher's without me, do you?"

"Of course not!" Emma said. "Besides, I'm practically in the band now."

"You've only practiced with them three times," Derek pointed out.

Emma frowned at him but let the statement slide. "Yes, I'll drop you off, Crystal. It's kind of exciting that she's talking to you again. Do you want us to come with you?"

"No." I shook my head. "It sounded like she wanted it to be just me and her."

"Okay," Emma agreed with a look of worry in her eyes. "You can text or call me when you're done, and I'll come get you."

When I exited the car, I nervously shifted my backpack on my shoulder and took a deep breath as I entered the mall. I was excited to talk to Sage again, but I was scared of what she had to say to me. I was sure she still didn't believe me, so warning her about her death was off the table.

I scanned the tables and restaurant lines for Sage, but I didn't see her. Maybe she wasn't there yet. I was headed toward an empty table and about to sit down when I caught a glimpse of auburn hair the color of Sage's. She looked up to meet my eyes as I made my way over to her.

"Hey," I greeted, slinging my backpack strap over the chair across from her.

Sage offered a smile, but it was the nervous type she

always had. "So, uh, what type of food are you in the mood for?"

I scanned the restaurant signs. "Chinese?"

I put my backpack back on as we made our way into the line, thankful that I had a few dollars from babysitting stashed away in it. I knew there had to be a reason Sage invited me here, like she wanted to talk about something, but all we could do was make small talk—like what kind of chicken we should order—until we got back to our table. I suspected she was too nervous to start talking, and I was already covered in a thin sheen of sweat anticipating what it could be about.

After a few bites and complete silence, I finally set my chopsticks down. "Did you want to talk about something?"

"Huh?" Sage looked up from her food.

"I guess I can't figure out why you invited me here," I admitted.

Sage gave a long sigh, the kind of sigh you make when you're trying to calm your nerves. She set down her own chopsticks and tugged on her sleeves until they were balled into her fists. She wiped at her nose with the back of her hand. "You're right. I do want to talk to you about something, but it's just really hard for me."

"You can tell me anything."

"Isn't that weird?" Sage said, catching me off guard. What did she mean? "The thing is, I know I can talk to you about anything, and that's crazy. We've only known each other for two weeks. I've been to therapist after therapist, and I couldn't talk to any of them. And then you . . . But then you said those things about my family . . ."

"Sage," I interrupted. "I'm sorry about that. I—"

"No, it's okay. It really is." She picked up her chopsticks again and poked at her rice. "I should be the one apologizing about the way I treated you." She bit into a piece of chicken.

"Thank you," I said, twisting some noodles around my chopsticks.

Sage swallowed. "Who's to say you're not telling the truth?"

I nearly choked, but I forced the noodles down my throat without a problem. "Are you saying you believe me?"

Sage shrugged as she shifted the rice around on her plate. "I'm not saying that. I don't know what to believe. Remember how I told you I thought I saw my family after they died?"

I nodded.

"Well, I've been thinking a lot about it, and what if I *did* see them?" Sage paused for a moment. "You didn't call me crazy when I said that, so I just feel pretty terrible about calling you crazy. Besides, Robin's been talking some sense into me." She gave a bit of forced laugh.

"Yeah, he's pretty good at knowing what to say."

An awkward silence filled the air between us while we each dug into our food.

"So," I finally said. "What was it you really wanted

to talk to me about?"

Sage gave an exhale through her mouth as if preparing herself. "So, I thought a lot about what you said. At first, I was really scared."

"Of what?" I asked when she paused.

"I—I guess I was scared you knew too much about me. I'm really good at shutting people out." Sage rubbed at her eye nervously. "You probably picked up on that."

I nodded and offered a sheepish smile.

"But like I said," she continued, "I have this weird feeling that I can trust you. My therapist says that if I can't open up to her, I should at least talk to someone. She tried to get me to write in a journal, but I just couldn't do it. Like, what if someone found it?" She sniffled and took another bite of rice. When she swallowed, she spoke again. "So, I figured I'd take a stab at talking to you."

A little part of my heart fluttered, touched that she trusted me enough to talk to me. I listened quietly and chewed slowly as she spoke.

"There are a few things you should probably know about me. You already know that my parents and sister died. But that's just one of my issues. When I was little, my uncle used to live with us." She pressed her lips together and looked around to make sure no one was listening. She lowered her voice. "He used to . . . do stuff to me." Her eyes shifted nervously but wouldn't look at me.

It took me a few moments to realize that I wasn't supposed to know this already. "I'm so sorry," I told her honestly.

"No, it's okay. Really. I was doing fine until my parents died. I mean, my dad always made me feel safe. But now that he's gone . . ." Sage twisted her sleeves nervously in her hands. She finally looked into my eyes, her own brimming with tears that threatened to pour over the threshold. "I don't feel safe anymore."

"Oh, Sage," I said quietly. This time when I reached over to touch her hand that now rested on the table, it wasn't awkward. But the moment I touched her, something changed. A sickening feeling overcame me. It felt like my insides were twisting and my guts were trying to force their way out of my throat. A tightening sensation rose to my eyes, and my nose tingled. Hairs stood up on the back of my neck.

I pulled away from Sage, almost too quickly. "I know how you feel," I told her, but I knew she had no idea how much truth there was to that statement.

Sage forced a smile, returning her hands back into her lap. "That's sweet, but I know you're just trying to make me feel better." She took another deep breath. "After my dad died, the nightmares of my uncle came back. That's why I didn't fight living with Anna and Brian—my mom's sister and her husband. I actually *wanted* to live with them because I felt I needed someone there to protect me. My therapist already knows all this, but what she doesn't know is something that terrifies me more than anything else."

"What is it?" I asked in a near whisper.

"I—" Sage paused like she wasn't sure whether to tell me or not. She stole another nervous glance around the food court.

"You can tell me," I assured her.

She bit her lip as if it was the only way to stifle the tears. Finally, her eyes locked on mine. "Sometimes I think I see him."

I drew in a sharp breath.

"Sometimes I think I'm going crazy," Sage admitted, rubbing the back of her hand at her eyes to wipe away tears she was trying so hard to hold back. "I don't know—maybe I am going crazy. Other times, I'm scared he's come back. Like, now that my dad's gone, he's coming to get his revenge, like he's still mad that I told my parents about him."

I didn't know what to make of this. If she was seeing her uncle—if he was stalking her—then that would definitely mean she was in danger from him.

"Where have you seen him?" I asked.

She shrugged. "Just around. I don't know. Once I thought I saw him when I was at the grocery store with my aunt. Once I thought I saw him driving down our street." She paused for a second and tilted her head in thought. "Actually, the day I met you, I thought I saw him on the bus on the way to work. But I don't know. I could be imagining things."

My heart sank, and I tried to picture what she was

going through. Then something clicked. *That's* what she was scared of the first day. I took just a split second to absorb this, and then worry filled my mind. If her uncle was stalking her, could he be out for blood?

"I believe you, Sage."

"Really?" she asked, raising her head and wiping her eye for the last time.

"I really do, but Sage, why haven't you told anyone? You should at least call the police."

She shook her head. "I would, but . . ." She hesitated like she had more secrets to tell and wasn't sure about whether to share them or not. "I'm not sure yet if I'm actually seeing him or if I'm just crazy."

If she wasn't willing to call the police, and I was still pretty sure I couldn't tell her when she was going to die, then what could I do? Maybe if I could change the course of the future . . .

"You know what I think you need?" I asked her.

"What's that?"

"I think you need to relax. That way, you'll be able to think more clearly, and you'll really know if you're imagining it or not. Why not hang out with us again? We can keep you safe." I smiled at her, hoping she'd believe me. I tried convincing myself of this at the same time. Could I really keep her safe?

"You, Robin, Emma, all you guys? You really think you can keep me safe?"

"It's better than being alone, isn't it?"

Sage shook her head. "I don't think any of you

understand how messed up I am."

"Well, we're willing to help. We could go back to Asher's and listen to them finish up practice. And you know what? They're playing again in two weeks at my mom's wedding. You should come to that, too."

"Really?" Sage said with a half-smile. "You're inviting me to your mom's wedding?"

"Why not? There will be a buffet and dancing," I added, hoping these extra perks might convince her.

"But you already have it all planned."

"Sage, it's fine. We're not super formal people. So, will you come?"

She sighed. "I'd have to take off work again, and I don't know what my boss will say since I already took a day off to go to Troy's birthday party."

"You could call it research," I quickly suggested. "Tell your boss you were invited to a client's wedding and you thought it would be a great opportunity to see how successful it was and to market the bridal shop."

Please say yes, I chanted in my head. If she said yes, it'd be my ticket to helping her. Then she'd be far away from her uncle or whatever it was that was supposed to cause her death. Plus, she'd be by my side all day, and I wouldn't have to miss my mom's wedding. *Please say yes*.

Sage's half-smile grew wider. "You don't realize how sweet you are, Crystal. I honestly would love to be there. I'll do my best to get off work."

I was so excited that I actually jumped out of my

chair and gave her a hug.

Sage laughed. "What are you so excited about?"

That you're going to survive! I thought. Instead, I shrugged. "I'm just happy we're friends."

Sage's smile was a genuine one this time. "Yeah, we really are, aren't we?" After a pause, she spoke again. "You won't tell anyone, will you?"

I tensed for a moment. My friends already knew most of it. But they didn't know about Sage thinking she saw her uncle, and she trusted me enough not to tell. I couldn't betray her trust.

I shook my head. "I won't say anything."

***

After Sage agreed to come my mom's wedding, I finally felt like I could relax. We caught a bus from the mall and walked the few blocks from the bus stop to Asher's.

"This is it," I told Robin after the band finished practicing and Sage had left.

"What do you mean?" he asked.

"She agreed to come to the wedding. This is how I save her, isn't it? I changed the course of the future. She'll be safe now." I took a breath. "Right?" I added.

Honestly, I wasn't entirely sure. What if it was some type of self-fulfilling prophecy and I was somehow going to *cause* it? No. That couldn't be right. There wouldn't be anything dangerous at the wedding.

Robin answered my question with a smile. "I think there's a good chance of it. You just have fun at the wedding, okay? I'll keep an eye on Sage."

"Really? Thank you so much!" I threw my arms around his neck and placed a kiss on his lips. My nerves were finally beginning to ease.

"Crystal," Emma interrupted, "are you ready to go?"

"Yep!" I bounced up the stairs excitedly. "I'll see you Thursday, Robin. Bye!"

"What are you so excited about?" Emma asked as we headed toward the car.

I didn't answer for a moment as I thought about it. "I just have a feeling that everything's going to be alright."

Emma narrowed her eyes at me in thought.

"What?"

She sighed. "Just don't get too excited. It may not turn out to be all rainbows and butterflies."

Emma's words put a halt to my excitement. Did she know something I didn't?

19

The week passed by almost normally. I didn't have any prophetic visions, but Emma and I kept up with our regular psychic sessions. We continued visiting Robin's band, thanks to Emma being a part of it now. I almost didn't even worry about Sage since she was showing up to band practices, and I finally felt like I'd sorted things out with her. Now it was just a waiting game. Homework, babysitting, and studying my psychic abilities took up most of my time, but as the wedding day neared, I spent more time talking to Mom about last-minute details.

The night before the wedding had me more nervous than I'd been the previous week. The rehearsal dinner went well without a single hiccup, so I wasn't scared about walking down the aisle or anything. What

I was scared about was whether or not my plan was going to work.

I stripped off the dress I'd worn to the rehearsal dinner I'd just returned from, took a shower, and changed into my pajamas. The hot water did little to soothe my worry.

"Mom?" I asked, knocking on her door.

She emerged a moment later dressed in a bath robe. "Yes?"

"Can I talk to you in my room for a moment?" I asked, spotting Teddy behind her. He was propped up on the bed reading a book.

"Sure."

Mom and I crossed the hall to my bedroom and both took a seat on my bed.

"What is it, sweetie? You look worried."

I forced a smile that came off genuine. "No, I'm fine. I just don't really know what to expect tomorrow. Part of me is sure Sage is going to be okay. But then there's a part of me that says it's all going down in flames tomorrow. I don't know which part is the psychic part."

My mom laughed. "That's always tough."

"Anyway," I sighed, "I just wanted to tell you that no matter what happens, I don't want you to worry."

My mom eyed me. "Do you know something I don't?"

The truth was, I did, but I'd promised to keep Sage's confession about her uncle secret. I wanted to open up to my mom about it because I still wasn't entirely sure if

Sage was just being paranoid or not, but I promised Sage I wouldn't tell.

"No," I lied. I managed to keep a completely serious face without a single twitch of my eyebrow. "I'm just saying that this is your *wedding* day. If something *did* go wrong, I wouldn't want you postponing something or doing anything that would make you miss out on your special day."

My mom took a strand of my long blonde hair and tucked it behind my ear. "Maybe we *should* have rescheduled."

"No!" I said almost too quickly. "That's what I'm talking about. I don't want my abilities to get in the way of things like this. Besides, how much would that have mattered?"

My mom twisted her lips in thought. "You realize that I'm going to worry about you whether something happens to Sage or not."

I smiled and nodded. "Yeah, you probably are."

"I'll be worrying about her, too, but cancelling it won't change your prophecy."

"Are you sure?" I asked half-jokingly, even though I agreed with her. There simply wasn't anything she could do.

"If it's what you want, I'll give you some space," she told me.

"Promise?" I didn't know why I was asking her this. I didn't even expect something bad to happen, but now that we were discussing it, it made the possibility a reality in my head.

"I'll try." She smiled.

"Okay. Now go get your beauty rest." I pushed at her playfully.

She headed toward the door, but right before she shut it, she said, "I love you, Crystal." Her tone conveyed true worry, as if she thought this was the last time she was going to see me. But I was going to be fine, wasn't I?

"I love you, too, Mom."

Are you going to be alright, Sage? I wondered after my mom shut my bedroom door. I took a deep breath. *Only time will tell.* Just to be sure I wasn't missing anything, I stretched out on my yoga mat and channeled my energy. *Sage is going to be safe, right? I mean she has to be. I can't fail her.*

I took deep, long breaths as I focused my energy on my fingertips to clear my mind. I couldn't help it when my mind raced with the possibilities.

Was inviting Sage to my mom's wedding the best idea? What if I'm wrong about the entire prophecy? What if this isn't when Sage is supposed to die? But if her uncle is stalking her, he might come to the wedding. What if her uncle finds her?

The idea of Sage's uncle finding her played through my mind, almost like the thought was mocking me. Had I been ignoring his involvement for too long? Alan was the one thing in all this that felt completely out of my control. I didn't even know much about him. Should I have told Teddy? He may have been able to help make sure Sage wasn't being stalked. But Sage told me not to tell. Was that a mistake?

So many worries flooded my mind.

"Daddy," I called out, my eyes still closed and my legs crossed on the mat. While I didn't know if he could even hear me, it eased my nerves a little to believe he could. "I need help," I whispered. "I need to know that Sage is going to be safe tomorrow. If her uncle is somewhere nearby . . . Well, I just need to know that I'll be able to save her. Please send me some sort of sign so I know what to look out for, so I can save her like Melissa asked."

It was already super late, but I sat silent for another hour or so. Much of my anxiety subsided, but nothing profound came to me. I decided to have a go at my crystal ball, hoping it would show me something that would help guide me in the day ahead.

I situated myself at my desk and relaxed enough that glowing colors swirled within the ball almost instantly. I only had to remind myself once to go into it with no expectations.

The swirling colors turned to fire like they had last time. Just like last time, the flames transformed into a deep red and took the shape of fingers. A hand lay limp in the crystal ball, floating there without a backdrop or surroundings to tell me *where* this would happen. Even as the image faded, I managed to keep most of my anxiety from rising back up in my chest. I closed my eyes and took a deep breath, letting the rest of my nerves fall away.

I can do this, I told myself.

I wasn't entirely sure what the image meant. Did it mean Sage was still going to die? Or was the ball just trying to deliver my still unanswered question: *how* was Sage supposed to die?

I wasn't sure. The best I could do was crawl into bed and hope that the next day would run smoothly. Before I slipped under the covers, I dug around in my book bag and pulled out the picture of Alan.

Are you dangerous? I pondered. I studied his face and wondered about him until I fell asleep.

***

A man balanced on a rooftop, arranging new shingles before nailing them in place. Sweat glistened off his back, and his brown hair – that shone slightly red in the sunlight – stuck to the back of his neck. A few other guys milled around atop the roof.

"Carl," a man called from the ground, but Carl couldn't hear him over the noise of his nail gun. "Carl," the man called louder.

Carl stopped and turned to the man on the ground. His waterfall of hair fell to his chin and concealed his face.

The man on the ground motioned for Carl to come down, and he did as he was told.

"What is it, boss?" Carl asked with annoyance.

"You're supposed to be on break."

"And?" Carl challenged.

"I can't afford to pay you guys overtime. Besides," his boss said, gesturing to him, "you look like you could use a drink. I can't have guys passing out up on that roof."

"I'll be fine, boss." One could practically hear Carl gritting his teeth.

"Carl," his boss said sternly. "Take your break."

Carl let out a puff of air. "Fine."

He stalked off toward a white van and reached inside for a water bottle. After slamming the door, he leaned up against the side of the company vehicle. The big red logo advertised Sorensen Construction based out of Woodmont, Indiana.

Instead of drinking his water, Carl poured half the bottle over his head. Only when he pushed the hair out of his face did his appearance become clear.

***

I woke with a start. Even though his hair was longer and his eyes had become cold over the years, I still recognized him. I threw the covers off instantly without even bothering to see what time it was. I burst into my mom's room without thinking to knock.

"Teddy," I said breathlessly, although his room was only across the hall, so I wasn't sure why I was out of breath. All I could think was that I was *relieved,* and I knew I needed to act upon my dream quickly.

Teddy groaned and rubbed his eyes. I looked at the clock on my mom's nightstand. It was 5:30 in the morning.

"Crystal? What is it?" Teddy asked with a tired voice.

"I know where he is! I found him!"

My mother cleared her throat and sat up in bed. "Found who, sweetie?"

"I found Alan! He goes by the name Carl now, but it's him." I couldn't help but smile at my victory. I made my way fully into the room and plopped down on my mom's bed. "He's in Indiana, and he's working for this place called Sorensen Construction."

Teddy was already reaching for a pen and paper out of his bedside table. "Are you sure?"

"I'm sure," I answered confidently.

"Okay." Teddy dragged out the word as he wrote down the information. "I'll call Roger and have him contact the police down there and get this figured out. After all," Teddy said, turning to my mom with a smile, "I shouldn't be working today. It's my wedding day." He leaned in for a kiss.

"Yuck," I groaned. "Get a room."

My mom blushed and threw her pillow at my head. I ducked just in time, and it hit the wall behind me.

"Well, I guess there's no point in going back to bed," my mom said. "I'm too excited!" She bounced up and headed to the bathroom.

"You know what this means?" I asked Teddy since he was the only one around.

"What?"

"That everything's going to be okay! Since Sage's

uncle is in Indiana, she's safe. No one is going to hurt her. It's going to be a beautiful day and an amazing wedding!" I headed back toward my bedroom. Just as I was about to close my mom's bedroom door, I turned back. "Teddy?"

"Yeah?"

"Will you let me know what happens with Sage's uncle?"

He nodded. "I will."

"Okay, thanks."

20

"Crystal, has anyone told you how beautiful you look?" Diane raved.

I sat in front of a mirror at the salon, and the stylist had just finished curling my hair.

"I hope Robin tells her that all the time," Sophie said as another stylist twisted her curls into a bun. "Otherwise, you should ditch him, Crystal."

I laughed. "He does tell me that, and I'm not going to ditch him."

A sense of happiness filled my heart. My mom's marriage became more of a reality as the day wore on. There was the added perk that I'd texted Sage earlier and she told me she was still coming to the wedding. Everything was going great.

Mom, Sophie, Diane, and I laughed and joked until

we were in full hair and makeup. Once we were done, we drove to the hotel and piled the last of our supplies into a small event space. We were the only ones there so far, and we took this time to arrange last-minute decorations that we hadn't finished setting up after the rehearsal dinner last night. Since it wasn't a big wedding—and the hotel we were at didn't even have wedding planning services—it was all up to us to set everything up. Everything, that is, except the catered food and the music, which Robin's band was providing.

I stayed with my mom in the smaller of the two conference spaces where we were holding the actual ceremony. Diane and Sophie were taking care of decorations for the reception in the other event room.

Just as I was helping adjust the last of the tulle, Robin popped his head in the door.

"Hey," he said. "We're here to set up the band equipment."

I smiled and hopped down from the chair I was standing on. I greeted him with a hug and a small kiss.

"Eww. Get a room," my mom joked.

I rolled my eyes at her. It was the best I could do since I didn't have a pillow to throw at her head.

"Come on," I said, taking Robin's hand and exiting the room. "I'll show you where the other event space is."

"I've been texting Sage," Robin told me in the hallway. "She says she still plans on coming. Are you still feeling good about this?"

I nodded excitedly. "I," I started, looking around to

make sure no one was listening. "I have to tell you something." I pulled Robin down a secluded hallway and told him about my dream.

"Teddy didn't say yet if they caught the guy?"

I shook my head. "It's only been a few hours, and I haven't seen Teddy since this morning."

"Okay. Can you show me where to set up?"

"Oh, yeah. It's this way."

Emma and Derek showed up a few minutes later to help us. I carried in band equipment and set things up for a while until Diane told me it was time to get dressed. Mom, Sophie, Diane, and I piled into a private hotel room to finish getting ready.

A few people came and went from the room to congratulate my mom in private, including Teddy's mom, Gail, along with some of my mom's cousins who I didn't even know. After the greetings died down, I helped my mom into her dress, and Sophie attached her veil.

"Wow." I stood back from my mom to get a good look.

She gave me a grin that bordered somewhere between excited and nervous.

"I can't believe you're doing this again," Diane said.

I pulled my mom into a hug. "I'm so glad I get to be a part of it."

Just then, a knock rapped at the door. Sophie hopped up from the bed to answer it. My Grandma Ellen—my mom's mom—stood on the other side of it.

"Grandma!" I rushed over to give her a hug. I hadn't seen her in ages.

Grandma Ellen adjusted her glasses. "Crystal, is that you? You've gotten so big."

I rolled my eyes at her.

"Oh, Mom. Come here." My mom crossed the room to hug Grandma Ellen. Tears of happiness pricked at both their eyes, but they did their best to hold them back.

"You guys can't cry, because then I'll start crying," I complained.

"Well, why don't you go put your dress on?" Sophie suggested.

I locked myself in the bathroom for privacy, but when I pulled my dress off the hanger, a lump formed in my throat.

She'll take her last breath the next time you wear that dress.

This can't be it, I thought. *Sage is going to be alright.*

But how did I know? A sickening feeling hit my stomach, and I sat on the toilet for support. I held the lavender dress out in front of me. I didn't move for nearly a minute as Melissa's words echoed in my mind. After what seemed like several minutes of holding my breath, I stood and put the dress back on the hanger.

"Why aren't you dressed yet?" Sophie asked when I emerged from the bathroom. "What were you doing in there?"

"I'll be right back. I just don't want anyone seeing

me in my dress yet. One of you can get dressed first." And then I left the room.

I made my way down the hall to the room I knew the groomsmen were getting ready in. After I knocked, Robin answered.

"Can I talk to Teddy real quick?" I asked.

"Yeah, sure." Robin pulled the door open wider to invite me in. "Why aren't you dressed yet?"

Teddy turned from the mirror as he finished adjusting his tie. "Crystal, I'm glad you're here. I wanted to let you know that Roger called me back. Your anonymous tip was right. They picked Alan up this morning."

I let out a breath I didn't know I was holding. "That's great!" I threw my arms around Teddy's neck in excitement. "Sage really isn't in any danger, then." I had the confirmation I needed, and I knew now that Sage had just been paranoid about seeing her uncle. She was never in any true danger from him. "Oh," I said, turning back to Teddy. "Congratulations."

Moments later, I was back in the ladies' hotel room and was pulling my dress off the hanger again. Each time I saw it, those words repeated in my head.

She'll take her last breath the next time you wear that dress.

What if she was never in danger from her uncle? What if it was something else all along? I wondered.

I pulled my cell phone from my back pocket.

"Hello?" Sage's voice answered.

"Sage," I said with a breath of relief. How could I think she wasn't going to be safe? After all, I'd invited her to the wedding and changed the course of the future. When she came, I'd be able to keep an eye on her all day. "Are you okay?" I found myself asking.

"Yeah, I'm fine. Why?"

"You're still coming, right?"

"Yeah. Actually, I was just headed out the door. Your hotel is only a couple of bus stops away, so I'll be there soon."

A smile formed across my face. I *was* right. I did change the future. She was going to be okay. "Okay. I will see you soon."

"Okay. Bye."

Once I hung up, I finally relaxed. I slunk down onto the closed toilet lid and took a few deep breaths.

A knock at the door pulled me to full attention. "Crystal," Diane said through the door, "you should be dressed already. Guests are arriving!"

I pulled the door open with my dress still in my hands. By now, my grandma was already gone, so it was just my mom and her bridesmaids in the room.

"This dress," I said, holding it out as if that explained everything I wanted to say.

They all looked at me quizzically.

"You guys think Sage is going to be okay, right?" Why was I bringing this up, anyway? I mentally scolded myself. It was my mom's special day. She shouldn't be worrying about things like this.

My mom made her way over to me and gave me a hug. "Honestly? Yes, I do think she's going to be okay. She has you on her side. Shall I also add that you changed things? Without you, she wouldn't be coming to the wedding. Without you, she'd be on a different course. And now, she's on one that leads to you. You've already changed her destiny by becoming her friend."

I closed my eyes and took a deep breath, absorbing my mother's confidence the best I could.

Sophie squeezed my hand for encouragement.

"Okay. I'll go get dressed now." I locked the bathroom door behind me for a third time and stripped down. I pulled the dress up over my hips and managed to reach the zipper this time. It hugged my body the same way it had the first time.

I emerged from the bathroom to find my mom and her best friends smiling at me.

"You look great, Crystal," my mom said, pulling me into a hug. Jeez. There were so many hugs going around today. After a moment, Sophie and Diane joined us, and we ended up in a group hug.

The ceremony grew closer, and we finished up last-minute preparations. Just as I was placing my pearl earrings in my ears, another knock came at the door.

This time, Grandpa Ed came in. "Are you ready to walk down the aisle?" he asked.

My mom nodded, though she appeared at a loss for words.

Grandpa kissed her on the cheek. "I'm so proud of

you."

She wiped at her eye carefully as to not mess up her makeup. "I know, Dad."

Grandpa checked his watch. "It's just about time."

My mom gave another one of those nervous but excited grins.

"Crystal, don't forget your shoes." Diane handed me my sparkly flats and my bouquet. This was it.

After a few more minutes of talking with my Grandpa and waiting for the ceremony start time to approach, we made our way downstairs. I gripped onto my owl necklace the whole way down.

"Crystal," Robin said when he saw me. He spoke in a near whisper so that only the two of us could hear. "I don't mean to freak you out, but I haven't seen Sage yet."

"What?" I nearly shouted.

Robin's dad gave me a stern look as if to tell me to be quiet.

My heart nearly fell out of my chest. The ceremony was about to start. Sage should be here by now.

"Are you sure?" I asked.

Robin nodded nervously. "I've been keeping an eye out for her, and I tried to text and call her, but she isn't answering anymore."

My face grew hot as I thought about the possibilities. *This can't be happening. I had to put on the damn dress.*

I stepped around the corner and peeked into the

ceremony room.

"Crystal," Diane scolded. "What are you doing?"

Robin quietly explained to her as my eyes scanned the crowd. With Sage's auburn hair, it should be easy to pick her out of such a small crowd, but not a single strand of red hair stuck out. Robin was right. Sage was missing.

21

"Do you have your phone on you?" I asked Robin.

"Yeah." He handed it to me.

His father gave another look of disapproval.

"It's on silent," Robin explained, like that would make his dad approve of him having it during the ceremony.

I found Sage's number in Robin's contacts and pressed the call button. My pulse increased with every ring. *Pick up, Sage,* I thought. When it went to voicemail, I felt like my entire world was collapsing around me. This was it. My worst nightmare. I'd failed her.

I froze so still that the phone dropped from my hand. I didn't even remember to breathe until Robin gripped my shoulders. I was sure it was the only thing keeping me from sinking to my knees.

"Crystal." Robin's voice made me feel stable again.

When the wooziness in my head finally cleared, I knew I had no other choice. I grabbed Robin's hand.

"Crystal, what's going on?" Sophie asked.

I turned back without slowing my step. "It's Sage."

"Crystal," Sophie stopped me. She quickly closed the distance between us and grabbed my wrist. "You can't go by yourself. We should come with you."

"No," I insisted without really thinking about it. "You guys told me this was *my* mission."

"That doesn't mean you should go alone."

My gaze shifted between Sophie's eyes. "Everyone keeps saying that I need to put more faith in my abilities. If *you* believe in my abilities, you'll let me do this myself, and you won't worry about me."

Sophie's eyes softened in defeat. "We do believe in you."

"Then you have nothing to worry about."

She finally released her grip on my wrist.

My mom was still hiding around the corner with my grandpa so that no one would see her before the ceremony. I called back to Sophie. "When Mom asks, tell her that she promised, okay?"

"Promised what?" Sophie raised her voice as I distanced myself from her.

"She'll know. Don't wait around or worry about me. Have fun."

Robin and I escaped into the sunlight and raced toward his car. He didn't waste a second and already had his keys out and the door unlocked before my hand even touched the handle.

"Where to?" Robin asked quickly with a wavering tone.

"I have no idea," I admitted. Robin was already pulling out of the parking lot. "Last she told me, she was headed out the door. What if she never made it that far?"

"You think something happened while she was at home?"

"I don't know, but that's my best bet right now. Do you know where she lives?"

"Luckily, yes. I had to drop off a homework assignment one time when she was sick from school. It's not far."

I couldn't sit still on the short ride to her house. Robin was right. It wasn't far, but the slow traffic made it feel like the car ride stretched into eternity.

"I could walk faster than this," I complained nervously, but when I looked out the window at the people on the sidewalk, it was clear we were traveling faster than any other method. The seconds ticked by, and my mind raced with the possibilities.

What happened to her? Is she still okay? Why did I have to put on the dress? I was right. It sealed in her fate. It was self-fulfilling. How could I have been so wrong about this? Is it her uncle? Has he come for revenge? No. That doesn't even make sense. He was caught this morning, and even if he did escape custody somehow, he couldn't have made it here in time.

We finally pulled up to Sage's house. Robin was driving so fast that when he slammed on the brakes, I had to brace myself against the dashboard. I was already out of the car before he shut off the engine.

I raced up the walkway and pounded on the door. Sage's aunt—I assumed—answered the door. "Sage," I said breathlessly because that was all I could manage to spit out. I took a deep breath. "Is she here?"

The woman's eyebrows furrowed in confusion. "She left quite a while ago. She told us she was spending time with Robin again." Her eyes moved past me and locked on Robin. "Robin," she said in surprise. "Isn't Sage with you? We wouldn't have let her go out if she was going somewhere else."

Robin reached the door and stood next to me. "That's why we're here, Anna. Sage *was* supposed to meet up with us at my uncle's wedding, but she's not there. We were worried and came to check on her."

A man came up behind Anna. "I knew she was up to no good," he mumbled. This must have been Sage's uncle Brian. I remembered her telling me he had a "suck-it-up" attitude.

"Hey," I defended. I was surprised when my voice came out loud, but I was too scared for Sage to lower my tone. "Sage isn't *trouble*. She's *in* trouble. She's staying with you so that she feels *safe,* and now she's not. She's not safe." I covered my face with my hands because it was all just too much. A wary breath escaped my lips. Everyone else was too stunned to say anything. "Oh, god, Robin. It's my fault." I dropped my hands and looked up at him.

"What are you talking about?" Sage's uncle asked. He stepped forward in a defensive stance. "Did you get Sage into trouble?"

"No," I answered honestly. "I—I think—I mean—I couldn't get her *out* of it."

"Crystal," Robin said in a tone I knew was supposed to soothe my nerves but didn't work. "Calm down." He turned to Anna. His voice was surprisingly even, something I couldn't imagine doing with the rate my heart was racing and my fingers were trembling. "Can you give us a minute?"

Anna and her husband eyed us.

"I'm sure Sage is okay," Robin told them. "It's just a stressful day for Crystal, and she's overreacting. Sage is probably already there and we just didn't see her." I could hear the lie in Robin's tone.

"Should we call the police?" Anna asked warily.

"She should be fine," Robin assured her. "Can you just give us a moment?"

Anna let the door fall shut as I turned and sank down onto the steps. I buried my face in my hands. Robin sat down next to me and pulled me into his arms. Tears were already falling down my cheeks.

"I've failed her," I managed to whisper.

"It's not over yet," Robin promised. "Let's think rationally for a minute."

I nearly laughed at the thought that I would be able

to think rationally at a time like this.

"Thanks to your abilities, we knew Sage was in danger. What if we can use them now to find her?"

"How?" I asked hopelessly.

"Well, let's see. What can you do? You can see ghosts."

"I can't control who I see or when."

"Okay. You can see the past."

"I don't know how that's going to help us." I finally pulled away from Robin and wiped the tears from my eyes with a sniffle. "I can see the future, too. Maybe if I could concentrate hard enough, I could see something about the future and hopefully change it."

Robin nodded. "That's a good idea, but do you know how to control those visions?"

I dropped my shoulders and shook my head. "I can also feel people's emotions, but I have to touch them. I guess I could feel Hope while she was in trouble even though she was far away, but I've never felt Sage like that. I don't think that will help us find her."

"Wait," Robin said excitedly. "Finding her." He looked at me like I should know exactly what he was talking about. "You can find things."

I gave him a look of disbelief. "Yeah, I find things like CDs and old books and socks and stuffed animals. I've never found a person."

"You found Sage's uncle," Robin pointed out.

I thought about this for a moment. "That could have just been a vision of the past or future."

"And you found Hope."

"That's because a ghost told me where to find her."

"But it worked. Both times."

I pressed my lips together in thought. "I usually need something to touch. Like, when Emma and I practice, I have to touch her hand to know where she hid the object."

"Okay, then we'll do that." Robin stood up.

"What do you mean?" I asked, but he was already knocking on the door again.

I could hear the voices behind it stop abruptly. No doubt they were discussing whether or not to call the cops. Anna answered after a few moments.

"Can we see Sage's room?" Robin asked.

Anna and her husband both looked at each other warily. "Brian?" she addressed him.

"Why do you need to see her room?" he asked.

"To see if there's something that could tell us if she was headed somewhere else." Everyone went silent for a few moments until Robin spoke again. "Look, I don't mean to offend anyone, but I've probably spent more time with Sage than anyone else here. I know her best. If there's something wrong, I should be able to find it in her room."

After another long silence, Brian finally nodded. I knew Robin hadn't talked to Sage often, but as Anna opened the door wider to invite us in, I felt it was an indication of how little her aunt and uncle knew about her.

Robin and I stepped into Sage's bedroom. It was small with an untidy twin bed against one wall and a dresser against another. The walls were bare as if the owner had only come to stay the night.

"We'll let you know if we find anything," Robin told Anna and Brian. His tone was one that asked for privacy once again.

"They seem to trust you," I said, but my heart sped up with the feeling that we were wasting time.

"I think I'm the only one of Sage's friends they've ever met," Robin admitted. "It was just that one time when I came to drop off her science homework, but I don't think she gets a lot of visitors. I thought they were her parents, though. She never mentioned her family's death to me."

I took a few deep breaths to calm my heartrate. I pushed farther into the room, hoping something would call out to me.

Robin was already opening and closing drawers. "What type of thing do you think you need?"

"It has to be something she touched recently and was probably special to her." I opened the top drawer of her dresser but found nothing except clothes.

Robin flipped through the dresses in her closet.

"A few weeks ago, Emma and I were practicing, and I did better when she hid something that was really special to me."

"Luna?" Robin guessed. He closed the closet door and headed toward the bed.

I blushed because the idea of still sleeping with a stuffed animal sounded childish. "Yeah," I admitted as I pulled the third drawer open. Nothing.

"So, do you think something like this would work?"

I turned around to face Robin, who was holding up a teddy bear.

"It was under the covers," he explained.

I shrugged. "I don't know if this is going to work at all, but I don't see anything else very personal lying around. We might as well try this." I grabbed the bear from his hands.

I again took one of my calming breaths as I situated myself on the bed and leaned my head against the wall. I closed my eyes and stroked the bear's soft fur. The bed shifted when Robin sat down, but he didn't say anything.

No expectations, I reminded myself. *Just breathe, stay calm.*

The task proved quite difficult, but I managed to slow my breathing enough that my hands stopped trembling. After what felt like a few minutes, I pulled the teddy bear to my face and inhaled its scent. It was weird that I recognized the fragrance, but it smelled like Sage. As soon as the aroma hit my nose, an image flashed behind my lids—a bloody image.

I sucked in a sharp breath and opened my eyes.

"What?" Robin asked. "What did you see?"

I shook my head. "Nothing useful yet, but I think

this might work. Give me another minute." I closed my eyes again and brought the bear back up to my face. In that moment, I took everything I'd learned in practice sessions with Emma and applied it to relaxing my body, relieving my anxiety, and letting go of expectations. I became so relaxed to the point where every nerve in my body went numb.

A floating sensation overcame me, and I had to open my eyes to make sure I was still in Sage's room. Oh, I was in her room alright, but it was all different. When I opened my eyes, I was looking down on my own body that sat on Sage's bed and clutched her teddy bear.

22

I gave myself a mere moment to take in the scene. I knew if I reacted badly, I'd be instantly snapped back into my body. Instead, I filled my mind with thoughts of Sage. I thought back to the first time I saw her at Special Day Bridal. I pictured us singing together with Emma in Asher's basement. I let her genuine smile and freckled nose fill my mind, and I pictured her pulling at her sleeves in the nervous manner she always did. And then I pulled up the memory of her playing saxophone.

I let the melody and the memory of her gorgeous tone play in my head. As the song continued, I began floating high above the house until I was taken above rooftops and guided over office buildings.

After the last notes of her solo played in my head, I restarted the memory, and it kept me pushing forward.

A forest of trees up ahead looked awkward butted up against man-made structures, but the melody pulled me closer, like what I sought was hidden in the trees. The tune grew louder, and the melody slowed as I descended toward a path.

In an instant, all the scenes I'd just passed whirled by me in a blur. My eyes shot open.

"What?" Robin asked, rushing to reach for my hand. "Did you find her?"

I stared wide-eyed at Robin because I couldn't believe what had just happened. Did I *astral travel*?

"I—I . . ." I stammered. "I don't know if she's alright, but I think she's in the trees. They're just that way." I pointed. "It's in the city. Not far."

Robin and I both sprang up from the bed. I let the teddy bear fall to the floor, and we rushed out of the room.

"What is it?" Anna called as we hurried to the car.

"It's fine," Robin assured her. "We'll let you know what happens. Sage is going to be alright."

"Are you sure?" I asked as soon as Robin drove off.

"What?" He glanced at me.

"Are you sure she's going to be alright?"

He squeezed my hand and nodded. "I told you that weeks ago. She has you on her side, remember?"

Anxiety built inside me. Were we too late? Robin turned a corner onto a busy street, slowing us down. I eyed the scene. Something about it seemed strangely familiar. Tall buildings lined the street, and groups of people milled along the sidewalk. A bus up ahead pulled to a stop, and people piled out.

I caught my breath, and I knew where I'd seen this street before. "Stop!"

"What?" Robin looked around and slowed the vehicle. "Do you see her?"

"No, but this is it!"

"What do you mean? I thought you said the park. That's where I'm going."

"She was running." I closed my eyes. Behind them, a scene played through my mind, and I found myself in Sage's body, as if I *was* her.

I climbed onto the bus and kept my head low. I didn't meet anyone's eyes as I took my seat and adjusted the strap on my purse nervously. I tugged at my cardigan's long sleeves and balled them into my fists. Hairs rose on the back of my neck. I swallowed, forcing down the lump rising in my throat. I situated closer to the window and angled myself toward it. Hopefully no one would want to sit by me.

The feeling that someone was watching me grew stronger as the bus ride grew longer. I glanced around nervously to the man in the seat next to me. He was fiddling with his phone and didn't even notice me. I subtly glanced to the back of the bus. Soft brown eyes met mine. I quickly turned away from him. Fear knotted in my chest.

That's not him, *I told myself.* But what if it is?

I stole another glance toward the back of the bus. His head was down now and hidden behind the chair in front of him, but the hair was the same shade of brown that had haunted my dreams for years. I trapped my lip in my teeth to bite back the bile rising in my throat. How did he find me? How long had he been following me? What would happen when he finally caught me?

I can't do it, *I told myself.* He can't catch me.

The bus pulled to a halt at the next stop. I couldn't waste another second. I slipped off the bus as quickly as I could and took off running. I glanced behind me to make sure he wasn't following. For a second, I was sure I saw his brown eyes through the crowd. I pushed forward harder, dodging people as I went.

When I rounded a corner, I broke free from the crowd. Up ahead stood a wall of trees offering me a hiding place.

He can't get to me. I can't face my nightmare in person. He's haunted me for too long. I won't give him that satisfaction.

I sprinted as fast as I could. Even as I found cover in the canopy, I still pushed forward.

My eyes sprung open. "The day at the paintball arena. It was warning me of *this.*"

"What do you mean?"

"She's there." I pointed to the road that had taken her to the trees.

Robin turned down the road and found a parking space alongside the curb. I kicked my door open before he even stopped, and I ran toward the trees the same way Sage had in my vision. My dress flew out around my legs, but I pressed forward. Robin didn't run much thanks to his leg, but I knew he was following me as quickly as he could.

As soon as I broke into the trees, I slowed. "I—I

don't know where I am," I spoke to thin air. I scanned the ground for any sign of footprints or broken twigs, but I had no experience tracking someone. My heart sank, and I fell to my knees.

Robin was at my side as soon as he caught up. "Crystal."

"I—I don't know what to do next. The trees are all I saw, but I don't know where she is in the trees."

Robin knelt down next to me, but he kept his eyes on the forest, no doubt searching for a sign of Sage.

"Where are we, anyway?" I asked. "What's a forest doing in the middle of the city?"

"Don't you know where we are?" he asked.

I looked at him stupidly.

"This is Bradshaw Park. That's what you were describing before. I thought you knew where we were going."

A feeling of confusion overcame me, but it only lasted for a moment. This is where Troy held his birthday party. It's where Sage and I took a walk together and where she called me crazy.

But it's also where Sage told me . . .

"I know where she is!" I exclaimed, rising so quickly that I got a head rush. I took off again after the dizziness passed. I didn't know where I was exactly since I'd never been on this edge of the park, but I knew Sage was somewhere in here, and if I could find the path, I knew exactly where she would be.

"Where? How?" Robin called behind me and spoke

between breaths.

"It's where Sage told me she comes to think." I breathed heavily. Since it'd been a while since volleyball season, I wasn't exactly in the best of shape. "It's where she feels safest."

We finally hit a path, and I started toward the center of the park.

"How do you know where you're going?" Robin asked.

"I don't," I admitted, but I pressed on. After only a few moments on the path, I saw the bridge up ahead. I sprinted faster, leaving Robin in my wake. *Please be okay, Sage.*

I dodged the bridge and headed to the edge of the water. I didn't calculate my momentum and ended up sliding down the steep bank. My wrist caught my fall, and it ached. Dirt coated my lavender dress, and my right foot fell into the water.

But I didn't care. That's because the sight I saw in front of me was more horrifying than anything I'd ever seen before. I'd seen things like this on TV before. I'd even seen flashes of blood in my mind. But none of it could prepare me for witnessing it in person with my own two eyes. Not even the sight of my father's casket when I was little could measure up to this gruesome moment. I immediately wanted to hurl.

Sage's body lay unmoving on the sandy platform. A bracelet of red liquid wound around her wrist and dispersed into her palm and off her fingers. The bloody image from my crystal ball came to life right before my eyes.

23

I rushed to Sage and fell into the sand next to her unmoving form. *We're too late,* was my first thought. My breathing grew heavy, and I took a split second to assess the scene. Sage's red cardigan was pulled up past her elbow. All along her right arm lay red marks, some fresh while others were already healing.

I could hardly believe what I was seeing. I'd always noticed how she nervously tugged at her sleeves, but what I didn't notice about it was that she was *always* wearing long sleeves. Now I knew why. She was hiding something beneath them.

Robin appeared next to me and pulled his suit coat off. He wrapped one of the sleeves around Sage's bloody wrist. Neither of us cared that it was a rental. Sage's life was all that mattered right now.

"Is she . . ." I couldn't finish my sentence. All I could do was stare at her pale, lifeless body and hold my breath.

Robin leaned down to her face. "No. She's still breathing."

"Should I call an ambulance?" I cried.

Robin shook his head and shifted, pulling Sage into his arms. Sage groaned slightly as Robin lifted her body. I breathed a sigh of relief. At least she was still with us, if only slightly.

"There's a hospital a block away," Robin told me. "It'll be faster if we took her there ourselves."

After Robin swooped Sage into his arms, I spotted a silver object in the sand. I snatched it up, along with her purse, and trailed behind him. "Are you sure you can carry her that far?" My throat felt like it was closing up, causing my voice to come out a few notes higher than normal. "What about your leg?"

"I can carry her, Crystal. She hardly weighs 110 pounds. We'll make it there. It's just a matter of getting there in time." Robin's words sent a nauseating sensation through my gut. He quickened his pace when he reached the path.

"Is she going to be okay? How far is the hospital? Do you need any help?" I couldn't stop babbling like a fool. Had I failed her?

Although we were walking as quickly as we could with Sage in Robin's arms, the stretch to the hospital seemed to drag on forever. As Robin said, it was only a block away, but every step we took closer to the hospital made it feel another mile away. Tears fell down my cheeks in fear for Sage.

I placed a hand on her head as we walked in hopes of comforting her if she was even mildly conscious. What I saw—or rather felt—twisted my gut.

Even as I touched her, I didn't think I understood what she was going through. I could feel her fear, and for a moment, I was able to see her uncle's face from her perspective, as a nightmare. The revolting feeling that hit me was nothing compared to the chronic fear Sage faced every day. In the moment my hand made contact with her head, I understood why she wanted to kill herself, why she wanted the nightmare to end.

The feeling was too overwhelming. I jerked my hand away almost immediately, like I'd just touched a hot stove.

Thoughts played through my mind as we neared the hospital. Why didn't I send someone to pick her up? Why didn't I mention her uncle and his arrest sooner? Then she wouldn't have been so scared.

Finally, we reached the door to the emergency room. The lady behind the counter noticed us immediately and came rushing to our aid with a wheelchair. As Robin set Sage down and helped balance her semi-conscious body in an upright position, I finally got a good look at her face. Her lips were drained of color, and her normally bright freckles seemed faded.

"What happened?" the lady asked.

"She lost a lot of blood," Robin said breathlessly.

The lady gazed down at the coat tied tightly around Sage's wrist. "How long ago?"

Robin and I exchanged a glance, but it was Robin whose head was clear enough to speak. "We don't know. We found her like this 10 minutes ago. Maybe sooner."

Another nurse was already by our side trying to calm us down. "Are either of you family?"

"No," Robin said, but his breathing sounded labored. I wasn't sure if it was from carrying Sage or because he was just as scared as I was.

Sage moaned, and I was instantly at her side.

An unfamiliar hand, undoubtedly the second nurse, grabbed at me. "Ma'am, we need to get her to a doctor."

I shook her off and gripped onto the wheelchair. "Sage?"

Sage forced her eyes open halfway and spoke my name in a hoarse whisper. "Crystal?"

Robin's hands were the ones that gripped onto my shoulder next. I managed to relax my hold on the wheelchair, and the first lady wheeled Sage away.

"I'm her friend," I cried after her, but the second nurse was pushing me back. "No," I struggled, raising my voice. "Sage needs me. Melissa said I was supposed to save her!"

Robin entwined his fingers through mine and pulled me into a one-armed hug. I nuzzled against his shoulder, and tears fell from my eyes.

"You already saved her," he told me, leading me to one of the chairs in the waiting room.

"You think that's it?" I finally asked after a brief silence, lifting my head to meet his gaze. "You think that's all I needed to do?"

"We've done all we can. What I don't understand is why she did it."

I went silent for a moment. Sage had confided in me about thinking she was seeing her uncle. I told her I believed her, but I could see now that she really was being paranoid. Still, I *did* promise not to tell anyone about that.

"She was just scared," I finally said. I shook my head during the silence that followed. "The stupid thing about all this is that if I hadn't invited her to the wedding, it may have not happened at all."

Robin pressed his lips together in thought. "I don't know about that."

"But then she never would have been on that bus, and she never would have run to the park, and never would have . . ." I couldn't finish over my sobs.

Robin hugged me tighter. "This could have happened at any time. The difference is that because it happened like *this*, today, you were able to stop it."

After a long silence, I spoke again in a small voice. "I saw her thoughts, Robin. She wasn't even thinking about the wedding. On some level, I think she forgot where she was headed and was so caught up in her fear.

She just wanted out."

"Where'd she get it, though?" he asked.

I looked at him. It took me a moment to realize he was talking about her weapon of choice. I still had her bag slung over my shoulder. I reached into it and pulled out the blade, twisting it around in my fingers. A string of blood ran along the length of it. Thank goodness I was sitting down because when I spotted the blood, I grew queasy.

An image flashed through my mind. Sage sat in the bath tub, and I watched the scene from her eyes as she spread soap across her leg. She reached for the razor and ran it across her skin. On the third stroke, it caught the end of her ankle. A single drop of blood fell into the water and dispersed in an almost artistic display.

The scene only lasted a second before my eyes focused on the room once again.

"Look at it." I held the blade out toward Robin. "It's from a bathroom razor. She tore it apart a few months ago."

"How do you know that?" He looked at me, but a moment later, his face softened as if to say, *Well, of course because you're psychic.*

"I just do."

Robin handed the blade back to me, and I slid it back safely into Sage's purse. The thought to bury it later and put the memories of Sage's attempt in the ground crossed my mind.

I excused myself briefly to go clean up. Luckily, I'd

only accumulated a bit of dirt, so it wasn't too hard to dust off, although I had to wipe down my wet shoe since sand had gathered on the sole and sides. When I emerged from the bathroom, I was as good as new—at least, I looked that way; I couldn't say the same about my aching heart.

As soon as I sat down, a man behind us cleared his throat. The second nurse from earlier stood beside him.

"Hi," he said with a smile. It didn't do much to cheer me up, but I knew it was supposed to be welcoming.

"Hello," I managed to croak out. I knew a series of questions was about to ensue.

Robin and I stood to meet the man's outstretched hand.

"I'm Cole DuBois, and I'm a social worker here at the hospital. I understand that you just came in with a female patient. In order to provide the proper care, I was wondering if I could ask you two a few questions about her before you leave."

"I don't want to leave," I told him. I glanced at Robin to make sure this was an appropriate response. He gave me a slight head nod. "I want to stay until I can talk to her." I *had* to. She had to know her uncle wasn't a threat. Maybe then she wouldn't be so scared.

After we answered Cole's questions—like how we knew Sage and what her home life was like—we remained in the waiting room.

Robin checked his cell while we waited. Apparently

Emma had already called four times, so Robin called her back. He explained most of the story to her, leaving out the part about me astral traveling in case anyone else overheard. Then he handed the phone to me.

I stared at it questioningly.

"She wants to talk to you," he explained, shoving the phone in my direction.

I took it warily before putting it to my face. "Hello?"

"Oh, good," Emma said with a breath of relief. "Your mom wants to talk to you."

Before I could say anything else, my mom's voice came over the line. "Crystal?"

"Hi, Mom. How was the ceremony?"

"We didn't start yet," she admitted.

"Mom! I told you to go ahead without me. You promised."

"That wouldn't be fair."

"You're wrong. It's unfair to you that Robin and I are keeping you and your guests waiting." Of course I wanted to be with my mom on her wedding day, but I couldn't leave now, not until I knew Sage was alright, and that could be hours from now. I also didn't want my mom rescheduling her wedding because of me. "Mom, seriously, don't worry about me."

"How can I not worry about you?" she asked.

I sighed. "Look, Mom, I can't leave Sage right now, but it's only fair that you get married today, so will you please stop keeping your guests waiting and walk down the aisle already?"

"Snarky, are we?"

"Well, it's the only way you'll get married today."

My mother sighed in defeat. "Okay, I'll get married. You're fine, though, right?"

I loved how much my mom cared. "I really am. I love you."

"I love you, too, sweetie," she told me before we said goodbye.

"I better call her aunt and uncle," Robin said after I handed his phone back to him.

"It looks like the hospital beat you to it." I pointed to a man seated away from us. Brian and Anna must have come while we were talking to Cole.

Robin rose from his seat and cleared his throat. Brian turned toward us.

"Hello," Brian greeted quietly, sorrow full in his voice. "I—" His voice cracked, and he swallowed to clear his throat. "I'm sorry. I'm just so mad at that girl right now." Brian said he was mad, but his demeanor showed he was more sad than anything. "I just don't get it. We take her in, put a roof over her head, and then she goes and pulls this stunt."

I wasn't even about to explain it to him. I knew he wouldn't get it.

"Anna is in there with Sage's therapist."

"Can we see her?" I asked, but I knew it was probably a dumb question. Of course I couldn't go in there while she was talking to her therapist, if, in fact, she was actually awake and talking.

We sat in the waiting room for another long while. The only thing I could do was worry about Sage.

"I feel like I could have done more," I told Robin when Brian stood and went to the restroom. "I should have sent you to go pick her up or something."

"Crystal, there's no point in worrying about what you should have done. Take a look at what you *did* do. You knew where to find her. You—and your abilities—saved her life. Do you have any idea how incredible you were today?"

I managed to crack a half a smile. He was right. I had *astral traveled* and managed to get to Sage before it was too late. A sense of pride washed over me at the thought that my abilities saved her, just like Robin had said I'd do all along.

I closed my eyes right there in the waiting room and whispered a short prayer to my father. I still wasn't sure if he was the one who had helped me, but it soothed my nerves nonetheless. "Thank you, Daddy," I said in such a low voice that even I could hardly hear it. I only hoped my words would find him.

Several hours had passed since we'd found Sage, but eventually, Anna and Sage's therapist approached us in the waiting room. Anna came to our side immediately. Her eyes were red like she'd been crying. Before I knew what was happening, she was pulling us both into a hug. "I just wanted to let you two know how thankful I am that you were there today. Your instinct was right, and if it wasn't for you, we may have lost her.

I've always known Sage had issues, but I didn't realize how bad. I'm just so happy to see she has friends like you."

All I could do was force a friendly smile in return. After we exchanged thank yous and you're welcomes, a nurse led us to Sage's room.

As soon as I walked in, I immediately rushed to her bedside. Her face was gaining its color back, but her expression was stone cold.

"You should have let me die," Sage whispered.

I looked toward Robin for help and then back to Sage. I grabbed onto her good hand for encouragement. "No, I couldn't do that."

Sage closed her eyes and went quiet for a moment. "I'm sorry I ruined your big day," she finally said. "My aunt and uncle, and my therapist, are really disappointed in me. I can't imagine how mad you are."

"I'm not mad."

She threw me a sideways glance. "If I had died, none of you would be bothered by me."

"You're not a bother, Sage," Robin assured her. He stood at the foot of her bed.

"I'm not trying to gain your sympathies. I just—sometimes I feel like I don't want to face things anymore. Sometimes I just want it all to go away."

I shifted and squeezed her hand tighter. "Sage, there's something I need to tell you, and I hope once I do, you'll change your mind."

She looked at me with an expression of confusion.

"Your uncle—not Brian, but Alan—they found him this morning. He was living under an alias, but he was arrested in Indiana earlier today."

Sage's eyes widened. "No. That's not possible. Remember what I told you?"

I glanced toward Robin nervously since he didn't know what she was talking about, but he remained calm.

"I've seen him. He was stalking me. That's why—why I had to do it. I had to get away."

"No, Sage. My mom's boyfriend—well, my step-dad—is a cop. He told me about the arrest. You're safe now."

Sage's body seemed to relax when I said this. She looked from me to Robin then back at me. "Really?" Tears welled up in her eyes. "You really mean it? I didn't see him on the bus?"

I shook my head. "No. You've always been safe with your aunt and uncle. You don't need to be afraid anymore. Besides," I glanced at Robin, "you have us."

A single tear fell down Sage's cheek. She spoke slowly and quietly like she was drained. "Oh, my god. I can't believe it. If what you're saying is true . . . That's such a relief." Sage gave a half-hearted laugh, but it came out sounding more like a grunt. "Now I feel like a total ass for dragging everyone into this." She paused for a moment. "How did the two of you know, anyway? They said you found me."

Robin and I exchanged a glance. Should I tell her

the whole truth?

"We noticed you weren't at the wedding," I started.

"Right," Sage interrupted. "I'm really sorry. When this all happened, it's like I forgot where I was going. I just ran. I sat under the bridge for a while, and then . . . well, you know the rest of the story. How'd you know I'd be there?"

"Well, when you weren't at the wedding, Robin and I went to find you. We stopped at your aunt's and uncle's, but then I remembered what you told me about the bridge, that it's the one place you felt safe."

Sage nodded in understanding. I guess I didn't have to scare her off with psychic stuff again.

"So, I guess you'll have to kill me now," I said playfully.

Sage's eyebrows came together in confusion, but after a moment, her face softened.

"I feel like I missed something," Robin said from the foot of the bed.

Sage explained. "I told her if she showed anyone the bridge, I'd have to kill her. But I'll give you a pass this time. I already attempted to take one life today."

Sage's last statement hung in the air uncomfortably, but I felt better that she was able to joke about it. After a while, Sage yawned and complained about being tired. I could tell it was her way of encouraging us to attend the rest of the reception.

"How long are they keeping you here?" I asked.

"They want to keep me overnight and make sure

I'm not going to harm myself again."

"Okay. We'll be back tomorrow to see how you're doing. Sleep well."

Robin and I walked back to his car and drove to the hotel. The whole while, I stared out the window with an inadvertent smile on my face. All my friends were right. With me on Sage's side, she'd always be safe.

24

When we entered the reception hall, Emma was singing into the microphone, and the floor was crowded with people dancing. Emma's eyes lit up, and she waved to us without missing a beat. I immediately found my way to my mom and her bridesmaids.

My mom squeezed me so tight I could barely breathe. "I was so worried about you."

"You said you wouldn't worry."

"I know. That was the only thing keeping me from calling the party off and going after you."

"It sounds like you almost did call it off. I'm glad you didn't," I told her.

"She made us stay back, too," Diane explained. "She told us she needed us more than you did. Given your talents, she was probably right." I knew Diane was just poking fun of my mom.

"That's not what I meant," my mom defended. "I have faith in you, Crystal."

"It was tough, but I managed. I'm sure Emma filled you in."

They all nodded.

"We'll be back to visit Sage tomorrow. For now, she's doing fine, so I guess I can finally relax."

The song ended and then shifted to a slow melody. I felt someone grab my hand and turned to find Robin. "Aren't you supposed to be singing?" I asked.

"I requested one more song so we could dance." Robin wrapped one arm around my waist and took the other in his hand. "Did I tell you yet how brave you were today?"

"This is only the fourteenth time," I joked.

Robin raised his eyebrows. "So, you've been keeping count?"

I laughed and waved goodbye to my mom and her friends as Robin pulled me across the dancefloor. It felt so good to laugh and be close to him like this, all the while knowing Sage was still breathing thanks to my abilities.

Derek approached us as we danced. "Hey, I heard what happened. I hope everything is alright."

"I think it is for now," I told him. "We're going to see Sage in the morning again."

"So, it appears all your mysteries are solved." Derek waved his hands in front of his face in a mystical manner.

I twisted my lips up in thought. "Not all of them."

He dropped his hands. "I'm not sure if I can help, then."

"Actually, you can. We still don't know anything about your birth parents."

Derek laughed but quickly relaxed. "You mean, Emma didn't tell you?"

I narrowed my eyes playfully at the band where Emma was singing. "No, she didn't tell me."

Derek sighed. "To be honest, I didn't want to know because I was scared of what I would find. I guess I just didn't want to ruin the image of my birth parents that I had in my head."

Just as I suspected, I thought to myself. *He really did care after all.*

"But I did it for Emma, you know. She's too curious. After convincing my mom I had a right to know, she finally told me. I felt kind of bad because she thought that since I'd found out I was adopted, I didn't think of her as my mom anymore." Derek shook his head like it was a ridiculous idea. "When I told her Emma was the one who wanted to know, she relaxed a little."

"So, what's the answer to the mystery?"

"As strange as it sounds, they died in a tornado. Apparently I was with my biological grandma when it happened, but my mom says it was a love story; they were found under a pile of rubble holding each other's hands."

"That's so sad."

Derek nodded. "I know, but it's romantic on one level, too, and knowing that, it kind of makes me feel better about it." He paused for a second. "Anyway, I'll let you guys dance. Then maybe Robin can get up there and give me a chance to dance with Emma."

Robin twirled me in circles, and we swayed to a slow melody. When I finally got a chance to listen to the tune, I realized it was familiar, but I couldn't place it until . . . "Oh, my gosh. Your band *learned* this song?"

When Robin and I were getting to know each other, we went to a Battle of the Bands concert. This was the song playing when we shared our first kiss. Granted, it was the result of a freaky psychic vision that led to our kissing, but still. "But this was that band's original song. How did you even remember?"

Robin shrugged. "I found the song on Youtube and sent it to everyone to practice, including Emma. We perform major pop songs. Why can't we play another band's songs as long as we don't claim it as our own?"

"Honestly? I don't care about copyright laws. This is downright romantic!"

"As romantic as dying holding hands?"

I pretended like I needed to think about it. "Almost."

Robin released my hand and wrapped both arms around my waist, pulling me in until our bodies were pressed together. He leaned his forehead down and rested it on mine. "You know what would be romantic?"

he whispered in a seductive voice.

I could smell his sweet spring scent and feel the warmth of his breath as it rushed across my face. It left my insides fluttering with anticipation. "What?" I whispered back.

And then Robin swooped down and pressed his lips to mine. He pulled my feet from the ground and twirled me around. Only when he set me down and released me did he speak again. "That."

I gripped onto his arms to steady myself and then wrapped my hands around his neck again.

One last time he came down to brush his lips across mine, and then the words I'd been waiting to hear for so long escaped his lips. "I love you, Crystal."

Happiness surged through me. "I love you, too, Robin."

***

That night, I stayed at Emma's house while Teddy and my mom got a hotel room before they flew out on their honeymoon in the morning. After sleeping in—thanks to a long night—I woke to realize I was so tired on the car ride home the night before that I'd forgotten to tell Emma all the details.

Emma yawned from her bed as I shifted from my spot on her floor.

"Emma, about yesterday, I realized I forgot to tell you something."

She rubbed her eyes and spoke with a yawn. "What do you mean?"

"After we went to Sage's aunt's and uncle's, I never told you how we actually found Sage."

Emma twisted her face in confusion. "Yeah, I was kind of wondering about that, but you were half asleep on the car ride home." Her demeanor instantly shifted, and she bounced onto her knees fully alert. Her eyes shined brightly, but she spoke at a million miles per hour. "How did you do it? Did you see the future? Did you find her with psychometry? Did you—"

I bit my lip to keep from letting a huge grin form across my face.

"What?" Emma asked. "Did you, like . . . I don't know. What else can you do?"

A blush rose to my cheeks, and I smiled proudly. "You're not going to believe me."

Emma shifted her gaze as if wondering what I could have possibly done. I expected her to continue guessing, but when she didn't say anything—thanks to being deep in thought—I spilled the beans.

"I astral traveled!"

Her jaw legitimately dropped. She didn't even blink. She just locked her eyes on mine, stunned. At some point, she realized that she had to actually *breathe,* so she shut her mouth and swallowed. "Are you sure?"

I nodded. "Well, we did all that research on it. It definitely felt like I was out of my body."

"Whoa. What did it feel like?"

"Kind of like I was flying."

"I knew I had a good feeling about astral travel."

"What?" I asked, but when I looked up at her, a cheesy grin spread across her face. I grabbed my pillow and threw it at her playfully. "You're good, but you're not that good."

Emma tossed her dark curls over her shoulder dramatically. "Oh, I'm *that* good."

All I could do was roll my eyes at her.

An hour later, Derek met up with us so we could go visit Sage together. Derek sat in the passenger seat silently as I filled him in on the details.

"That's all just so . . . unbelievable."

I bit my lip nervously. Did he really mean that?

"I mean, it's amazing." Derek finally shifted to look back at me. "I hate to abandon my whole belief system, Crystal, but unless you're lying to me, I can't think of any other explanation. And you obviously weren't lying." He pointed to my face. "Your eyebrow wasn't twitching the whole time."

My hand immediately flew up to my eyebrow. While he was right—I wasn't lying—I had gotten better about the whole eyebrow twitching thing lately.

Derek noticed my reaction and burst out laughing.

Once the laugher in the car died down, Emma spoke. "You know, maybe you don't have to change your belief system. I mean, you believe in an afterlife, Derek. Given that Crystal has seen ghosts and helped them cross over, she *knows* there's an afterlife."

This gave us all something to think about, and the car filled with silence.

"Do you think we should bring her a gift?" Derek asked as we neared the city. "Maybe a get-well card or a stuffed animal or something."

Emma gave Derek a look of disapproval. "She's not going to want a stuffed animal. Maybe we should have brought some of the leftover cake Sophie took home."

"I don't know," I said from the back seat. "I think a stuffed animal and a get-well card is a good idea."

"Crystal, she nearly died," Emma pointed out. "It's not like she's a kid with strep throat."

"Well, what do you suggest? Besides cake."

Derek and Emma went back and forth with ideas as we drove, but after a while, I figured I should call Robin and let him know we were on our way. I opened up my contact list, and there on the top sat a name pulled from my Facebook friends' list. Something he'd said a while back surfaced in my memory, and I instantly had the perfect idea on what to bring Sage. Even Emma had suggested the same thing weeks ago.

Maybe if she played again it would help. It could be like therapy or something, Emma had said.

I pulled up Andrew's profile on my phone and sent him a quick message, praying that he'd see it soon. Not even a minute later, he sent a message back agreeing to help me.

We stopped at Andrew's and Faith's house on the way to the hospital and then swung by to pick up Robin.

I talked to one of the nurses before she led us to Sage's room. She was wary of my plan at first, but Robin managed to work a bit of his charm and convince her.

When we walked into Sage's room, it seemed smaller with Emma and Derek along, but Sage looked to be doing a lot better. She was sitting upright in her bed and staring at the TV. She greeted us with a nearly genuine smile and pressed a button on the remote. The TV went silent.

"So, how was your mom's wedding?" Sage asked in a light tone that told me she was feeling better. "You know, after I ruined it."

"You didn't ruin it," I assured her. I blushed and looked over to Robin, remembering the way he'd told me he loved me the night before.

"What's that?" Sage asked, pointing to the case in my hand, the one I'd borrowed from Andrew.

I pulled it close to my chest despite it being a bit big. "Well, we wanted to bring you something, and we thought this might help you feel better."

"Is that what I think it is?"

I set the suitcase-sized case next to her on the bed and clicked it open. "If you think it's a saxophone, then you're right."

Sage's eyes lit up when she saw the horn. It was like watching a small child peering into a treasure chest. Her hand reached for it, but she pulled away at the last second as if she'd realized what she was doing.

"I can't," she said, shaking her head. "The hospital

wouldn't allow it."

Just then, Sage's nurse stepped into the room. "Actually, I just talked with the other patients in the hallway, and they'd be delighted to hear you play. Your friends say you're quite good."

Sage looked at each of us warily. "How did you even—I mean—where did you get it?"

"Remember Andrew?" I asked.

Sage nodded.

"Well, I remembered he said he played saxophone in the jazz band. I messaged him on the way here. He let us borrow it for you."

Sage looked down at the horn in wonder and then back to her nurse. "Are you sure?"

Her nurse nodded kindly.

Sage took a deep breath and then reached into the case to assemble the saxophone. "I don't even know what I'd play."

"Play your solo," Emma suggested.

Sage looked at her in confusion.

Emma sighed like the answer was obvious. "We watched a video of you playing a solo last year. Your eyes were on the director, so you obviously had it memorized."

Sage situated the saxophone in her hands. "I don't know if I remember it anymore."

"I still remember my last solo and ensemble piece on clarinet," I said. "You probably practiced a lot more than I did."

Sage placed the mouth piece to her lips but pulled it back out. A tear pricked at the side of one eye. "I can't believe you did this for me." Then she brought the horn back to her lips and breathed into it. Her hands moved across the keys, and the most beautiful tune I'd ever heard filled the room and echoed down the hallway.

As she played, I lifted my eyes to the ceiling and whispered a silent prayer to my father. "Thank you for helping me save her." A feeling of serenity washed over me, and I knew at that moment that even though I couldn't see the spirits helping me from the other side, they were always watching over me. "And thank you for helping me find the courage to face my own demons," I added.

Sage kept her eyes closed the entire time, concentrating on the notes. After just a few bars, a small crowd had formed outside her room. The intensity of the solo grew to near fierce proportions but then softened into a relaxing tune. Sage held out the last note with perfect tone. Applause filled the room, and Sage opened her eyes for the first time since starting the solo. More tears fell down her cheeks when she realized how many people had been listening.

"I forgot how much I loved it."

EPILOGUE

The summer heat left my mom and me fanning ourselves in the living room. I'd asked Teddy earlier if he wanted help fixing the air conditioning unit, but he insisted he could do it himself. It was a Saturday morning, and my mom and I had nothing better to do than fold up paper fans and blow air each other's way. It was actually fun since she'd brought her craft box out and we'd glued lace and other fun things to our fans.

"It's going to be a girl," I told my mom confidently.

She rolled her eyes at me but continued fanning my face. "How many times do we have to go over this? It's going to be a boy." She laid one hand on her still flat belly.

"I thought you couldn't see the future if it had to do with friends or family," I accused.

My mom just laughed. "I don't have to see the future. I'm a mother. Women know these things."

"So you knew I was going to be a girl?"

She nodded proudly.

Just then, the doorbell rang. We both exchanged a look of confusion since we weren't expecting anyone. Maybe Teddy finally decided to call a professional.

I rose from the couch and pulled the door open. Bright eyes and a freckled face stared back at me. The redhead wore a flattering green tank top that exposed her arms.

"Sage!" I cried in excitement, pulling her into an embrace. We'd stayed in touch since she was released from the hospital, but I hadn't seen her in a few weeks. "Come in. It's not any nicer in here, though." I opened the door wider so she could step inside.

"Sage," my mom greeted from the couch. "Want a fan?"

Sage eyed the fan, and an amused smile played at her lips. "No, I'm okay. I actually just came to give you this." She held out an envelope made of fine stationery.

"What's this?" I asked warily, taking it from her hands.

"Well, after everything that happened a few months back, my therapist and I got to talking seriously. I asked her if there were any music therapy programs around, and she said she hadn't heard of one in the area."

I peeled open the envelope as she spoke.

"So, she suggested we start one. We have a huge group of teens who come together once a week for music group therapy, and we're putting on a concert in a few weeks. I was really hoping you'd come. After everything you did for me, I just wanted to show you how much I appreciated it."

"That's so nice of you," I said, pulling the invitation out of the envelope.

"We've been working on winter-themed songs."

"Why winter?" I asked. "It's not even autumn yet."

Sage only smiled at me. That's when I finally looked down at the invite and noticed the title of the concert:

INSPIRED BY FROST

ABOUT THE AUTHOR

Alicia Rades is a USA Today bestselling author of young adult paranormal fiction with a love for supernatural stories set in the modern world. When she's not plotting out fiction novels, you can find her writing content for various websites or plowing her way through her never-ending reading list. Alicia holds a bachelor's degree in communications with an emphasis on professional writing.

Made in the USA
San Bernardino, CA
07 August 2017